Katinka

Herman Bang.

HERMAN BANG

Katinka

Translated from the Danish
by Tiina Nunnally

FJORD MODERN CLASSICS NO. 3

Fjord Press
Seattle
1990

Title of Danish edition: *Ved Vejen*
Originally published as part of *Stille Existenser* in 1886 by Det Schubotheske
Forlag, Copenhagen.

Grateful acknowledgment is given to the National Endowment for the Arts
and the Danish Ministry of Cultural Affairs for their generous support.

The translator wishes to thank Inge Rifbjerg for her invaluable assistance.

Published and distributed by:
Fjord Press
P.O. Box 16501
Seattle, Washington 98116
(206) 625-9363

Editor: Steven T. Murray
Cover design: Bonnie Smetts Graphic Design, Berkeley
Cover painting: Cheri O'Brien
Frontispiece and back cover photograph courtesty of the Royal Library,
    Copenhagen
Design & typography: Fjord Press, Seattle
Proofreading: Nete Leth
Printed by Malloy Lithographing, Ann Arbor

Library of Congress Cataloging in Publication Data:

Bang, Herman, 1857–1912.
    [Ved vejen. English]
    Katinka / Herman Bang; translated from the Danish by Tiina Nunnally.
        p.   cm. — (Fjord modern classics ; no. 3)
    Translation of: Ved vejen.
    ISBN 0-940242-47-8. — ISBN 0-940242-46-X (pbk.)
    I. Title.   II. Series.
PT8123.B3V413   1990   839.8'136 — dc20   90-45560

The paper used in this publication meets the minimum requirements of
American National Standard for Information Sciences — Permanence of
Paper for Printed Library Materials, ANSI Z39.48-184.   ∞

Printed in the United States of America
First edition

About the Author

Herman Bang (1857–1912) is one of the greatest Scandinavian writers of the 19th century, renowned for his impressionistic style and realistic portrayals of urban decadence and stultifying provincialism. Influenced by the works of Zola, Flaubert, and the Norwegian author Jonas Lie, Bang wrote his novels and short stories with meticulous attention to detail—it is the nuances of speech, the slightest gestures, the smallest minutiae of daily life that interest Bang and give his works their dramatic power.

And it is the "outsiders" of society who are Bang's main concern—the outcasts and misfits, or simply those whose sensitive nature puts them at odds with the average person. Bang himself was an outsider in turn-of-the-century Europe. Openly homosexual and an influential journalist who was constantly embroiled in controversy, Bang was well aware of the consequences of being "different." In 1880 his first novel, *Haabløse Slægter* (Hopeless Generations), was confiscated, judged degenerate and immoral. Scandal and turmoil followed him all his life.

Born on the island of Als in southern Denmark, Herman Bang was orphaned at a young age. His mother died of tuberculosis and his father, who was a pastor, succumbed to madness in the pulpit one day and later died in an asylum. As a youth, Bang's greatest love was the theater, and he was determined to become an actor—an ambition that was thwarted, however, by his apparent lack of talent, although he did achieve some success later on as a director. Instead, he turned

to journalism and built a considerable reputation for himself
as a literary critic, theater reviewer, and reporter on big-city
life in Copenhagen, often shocking his readers by revealing
the underside of society.

As a writer Herman Bang was equally controversial. His
impressionistic, almost cinematic style was far ahead of its
time. He seldom analyzes or describes; through dialogue and
action he draws the reader into his world and creates a sense of
immediacy. *Katinka,* with its spare, airy style and subtle
humor, is considered his masterpiece. Bang's contemporaries
largely failed to recognize the brilliance of his writing, but
future generations have acknowledged his greatness.

Herman Bang's death was as ironic and odd as the rest of
his life. After falling ill in a train on his way from Chicago to
California during a lecture tour, Bang died in a Mormon hos-
pital in Ogden, Utah.

Tiina Nunnally
Seattle, 1990

Katinka

Chapter One

The stationmaster changed his jacket for the train. "Damn, how time flies," he said, stretching his arms. He had been dozing a little over the accounts.

He lit the stub of a cigar and went out onto the platform. When he walked up and down like that, his clothes snug and his hands in both jacket pockets, you could still see the lieutenant in him. You could see it in his legs too, which were still bowed from the cavalry.

Five or six farm hands had appeared halfway down the station platform and were standing in a huddle and swaggering. The station hand dragged up the freight, a single green-painted chest that looked as if it had been dropped by the side of the road.

The pastor's daughter, tall as a Royal Guard, tore open the platform gate and came in.

The stationmaster clicked his heels together and greeted her.

"What does the young lady intend to do today?" he said. When the stationmaster was "on the platform," he conversed in the same tone of voice he had used in the old days in the cavalry, at the club dances in Næstved.

"Go for a walk," said the pastor's daughter. She made rather strange flapping gestures when she spoke, as if she meant to keep striking the person she was talking with. "By the way, Miss Abel is coming home."

"Already? From the city?"

"Well, yes . . ."

"And still nothing that sparkles?" The stationmaster wiggled the fingers of his right hand in the air, and the pastor's daughter laughed.

"There you have the family," she said. "I made my excuses and escaped from them."

The stationmaster greeted the Abel family, the widow and her eldest, Louise. They were accompanied by Miss Jensen. The widow looked resigned.

"Yes," she said, "I'm here to fetch my Little Ida."

Widow Abel took turns fetching her Louise and her Little Ida. Louise in the springtime and Little Ida in the fall.

They spent six weeks each time with an aunt in Copenhagen. "My sister, the councilor's wife," said Mrs. Abel. The councilor's wife resided on the fifth floor and made a living painting pictures on terracotta objects of storks standing on one leg. Mrs. Abel always sent her daughters off with the best of wishes.

She had been sending them off for ten years now.

"Oh, what letters we've received this time from Little Ida."

"Yes, what letters," said Miss Jensen.

"But it's better to have your little chicks at home," said Mrs. Abel, looking tenderly at Big Louise. Mrs. Abel had to dry her eyes at the thought.

The widow's little chicks spent the months they were home quarreling and sewing new trim on old dresses. To their mother they never said a word.

"How could anybody stand it in this backwater if they didn't have a family life?" said the widow.

Miss Jensen nodded.

Up toward the inn there were dogs barking, and a wagon rolled around the bend.

"It's Kiær's wagon," said the pastor's daughter. "What are they up to?" She crossed the platform toward the gate.

"Yes," said landowner Kiær, getting out of the wagon, "you might well ask . . . Madsen goes and gets typhus right at the worst time so a man has to arrange for a substitute by telegraph—and then the devil knows what kind of riffraff I'll get . . . He's on his way now."

Landowner Kiær stepped onto the platform.

"At least he's graduated from agricultural school—if that's any help—and with the highest marks. Oh well . . . Morning, Bai." The stationmaster received a handshake. "Don't suppose there are any rounds being served at your place? And your wife?"

"Oh yes, just fine. So you're picking up the foreman today."

"Yes—a horrible business—and right at the worst time."

"So—a new man in the neighborhood," says the pastor's daughter, swinging her arms as if giving him a box on the ear in advance. "That makes six and a half, counting little station hand Bentzen . . ."

The widow is in a frenzy. She had told her at home: Big Louise was not to go out with those prunella boots on.

Big Louise's "beauty" is in her feet . . . slender, aristocratic feet.

And she had told her . . .

Miss Louise was in the waiting room adjusting her bodice veil. The Misses Abel dressed in deeply cut bodices with a ruff, jet beads, and a veil.

Bai went around to the kitchen to tell his wife about the foreman. The pastor's daughter sat on the green-painted chest dangling her legs. She picked up her watch and looked at the station clock.

"God, that man is playing hard to get," she said.

Miss Jensen said, "Yes—the train does seem to be a few minutes delayed." Miss Jensen spoke with indescribable correctness, especially when she was talking to the pastor's daughter. She wasn't very fond of the pastor's daughter.

"That is not the tone used by my *étudiants*," she said to the widow. Miss Jensen was not very confident using foreign words.

"Oh, here comes that lovely woman." The pastor's daughter got up from the chest and raced across the platform toward Mrs. Bai, who had come out onto the stone steps. The pastor's daughter greeted her so heartily that it looked like a physical assault.

Mrs. Bai smiled calmly and let herself be kissed.

"Lord have mercy," said the pastor's daughter, "we're unexpectedly going to get a new rooster on the farm. There he is!"

They heard the rumble of the train in the distance and the loud clatter when it passed over the river bridge. Slowly it came huffing and swaying across the meadow.

The pastor's daughter and Mrs. Bai remained standing on the steps. The young lady had her arm around Mrs. Bai's waist.

"There's Ida Abel," said the pastor's daughter. "I can recognize her by her veil." A bordeaux-colored veil waved from a window.

The train stopped and the doors were thrown open and back. Mrs. Abel shrieked her hellos so loudly that the travelers in all the neighboring compartments came to the windows.

Little Ida peevishly pinched her mother's arm—she was still standing on the step.

"There's a gentleman on the train—coming here . . . Who is he?" It was like trying to stop a wheel with a stick.

Little Ida had stepped down. There was the gentleman. A blond-bearded, very sedate gentleman, who was taking hatboxes and cases out of a smoking compartment.

"And Aunt—Aunt Mi!" shrieked the widow.

"Shut up," muttered Little Ida irritably. "Where's Louise?"

Louise jumped up onto the steps in front of Mrs. Bai and the pastor's daughter as childishly as if her "beauty" were in her high-button shoes.

At the foot of the steps the foreman was introducing himself to Mr. Kiær.

"Yes, it's a hell of a mess—there lies Madsen—at the worst time. Well, we have to hope for the best." Mr. Kiær slapped the new foreman on the shoulder.

"God help us," said the pastor's daughter. "Quite an ordinary domestic animal."

The green-painted chest was inside, and the milk cans from the cooperative had been lugged out of the freight car. The train was starting to move off when a farmer shouted from a window. He didn't have a ticket.

The train conductor, a slender youth, stiff as a hussar in his elegant long jacket, signaled Bai with two fingers and leapt up onto the step.

The farmer kept on yelling and arguing with the conductor, who was still on the step.

And all the faces on the platform watched the train for a moment as it rolled away.

"Well, that's that," said the pastor's daughter. She went into the hallway with Mrs. Bai.

"My foreman, Mr. Huus," said Mr. Kiær to Bai, who was walking past. The three of them stood in silence for a moment.

Big Louise and Little Ida finally found each other and began kissing wildly in the middle of the doorway.

"Oh God," said the widow, "they haven't seen each other in six weeks."

"You're in luck, Mr. Huus," said Bai in his club-dance tone of voice. "You'll meet the ladies of the village right away. Ladies, may I introduce you?"

The Misses Abel stopped their kissing as if on command.

"The Misses Abel," said Mr. Bai. "Mr. Huus."

"Yes, I've just been fetching my youngest—from Copenhagen," said the widow, apropos of nothing.

"*Mrs.* Abel," said Mr. Bai.

Mr. Huus bowed.

"Miss Linde"—that was the pastor's daughter—"Mr. Huus."

The pastor's daughter nodded.

"And my wife," said Mr. Bai.

Mr. Huus said a few words and they all went in to get their baggage.

Landowner Kiær drove off with the foreman. The others walked. By the time they reached the road they had forgotten all about Miss Jensen.

She was standing and dreaming on the platform, leaning against a signal post.

"Miss Jensen," shouted the pastor's daughter from the road.

Miss Jensen gave a start. Miss Jensen always grew melancholy whenever she saw a train. She couldn't stand to see "something go away."

"Quite a nice person," said Mrs. Abel a little way down the road.

"A very ordinary foreman," said the pastor's daughter. She was walking arm in arm with Mrs. Bai. "He had nice hands."

The two little chicks walked behind, quarreling.

"Hey, Miss Jensen, what's your hurry?" said the pastor's daughter. Miss Jensen was leaping like a goat between the puddles in the road way up ahead. She was revealing a great deal of her maidenly legs because of the autumn dampness.

They walked past the little patch of woods. At the bend in the road, Mrs. Bai said farewell.

"Oh, how small and darling the lovely woman looks in that big shawl," said the pastor's daughter and threw herself at her again.

"Goodbye."

"Goo-ood-bye . . ."

"She sure doesn't waste any breath talking," said Little Ida.

The pastor's daughter was whistling.

"No—oh, there's the curate," said Mrs. Abel. "Good evening, Curate. Good evening."

The curate tipped his hat. "I just had to say hello to the returning daughter," he said. "Well, Miss—and your health?"

"Fine, thank you," said Miss Abel.

"And you have a rival now, Curate," said Mrs. Abel.

"Is that so? Where?"

"Kiær picked up his new foreman—quite an attractive person. Don't you think so, Miss Linde?"

"Well, yes . . ."

"First rate, Miss Linde?"

"F.F.," said the pastor's daughter.

The pastor's daughter and the curate always spoke in jargon whenever they were with strangers and never said a sensible word. They laughed so hard at their own inanities that they were just about to burst.

The pastor's daughter never went to church anymore when the curate was preaching, ever since one Sunday when she had almost made him laugh in the pulpit during the Lord's Prayer.

"Miss Jensen is taking off as if she had rockets lit in a certain place," said the curate.

Miss Jensen was still far ahead.

"Why, Andersen," Miss Linde hooted, "now you sound like a Holberg play."

They arrived at the parsonage, which was the oldest farm in the village, and the pastor's daughter and the curate said goodbye at the garden gate.

"Goodbye, Miss Jensen," shouted Miss Linde down the road. She received only a peep in reply.

"What was he like?" said the curate in the garden. Here his tone was totally different.

"Good Lord," said Miss Linde, "a very nice farmer."

In silence they walked side by side down through the garden.

"Well," said Miss Ida—the Abel family had caught up with Miss Jensen, who stood waiting on a dry spot—"I'm certain that he came to say hello to *me*."

They walked on for a while. Then Miss Jensen said, "There are so many kinds of people."

"Yes, there are," said Mrs. Abel.

"I have no desire to associate with that family," said Miss Jensen. "I'd rather go out of my way."

Miss Jensen had been going "out of her way" for a week. Ever since the pastor had said those *words . . .*

"Mrs. Abel," said Miss Jensen. "What is a single woman to do? I said that to the pastor: 'Pastor,' I said, 'you show an *interest* in the Free School . . . that's why parents send their children to the Free School.' And what did he say to me, Mrs. Abel? I won't talk to Pastor Linde about the stipend situation anymore. The parish council has taken away half of the stipend for my institute" (Miss Jensen pronounced it *instityoot*)— "*I* shall continue to do my duty—even if they take away the other half too. I refuse to discuss the stipend situation with Pastor Linde any longer."

The three women had turned down a little road that led up to the "farm," an old white building with two wings.

Widow Abel lived in the wing on the right; Miss Jensen's institute was in the one on the left.

"Ah, to have them both home again," said the widow. They said goodbye in the courtyard.

"Ugh," said Little Ida when they were inside, "the way you looked at the station—it was mortifying."

"I'd like to know how we're supposed to look," said Big Louise, who was loosening her veil in front of the mirror, "when *you're* the one with all the clothes."

The widow put on her slippers. There was no lining in her boots.

Miss Jensen finally managed to fish the key out of her pocket and let herself in. From the parlor the pug gave a few irritable yaps at his mistress and remained lying in his basket.

Miss Jensen took off her coat and sat down in a corner to cry.

She cried every time she was alone, ever since Pastor Linde had said those words.

"You show an interest in the school, Pastor," she had said, "that's why parents send their children to the Free School."

"I have to tell you, Miss Jensen, why parents send their children to the Free School—because Miss Sørensen knows her stuff." That's what the pastor had replied.

Miss Jensen had only confided "the words" to the innkeeper's wife.

"And what is a single woman to do, Madam Madsen?" she had said. "Woman's only defense is tears . . ."

Miss Jensen sat and cried in her corner. It began to grow dark, and finally she got up and went out to the kitchen.

She lit a kerosene stove and put the kettle on for tea. She placed a cloth over a corner of the kitchen table and put out bread and butter in front of the single plate.

But as she was doing this she would pause for long moments and think once more about the pastor's words.

The pug had followed her out and lain down on a pillow in front of his empty food dish.

Miss Jensen took the dish and filled it with white bread soaked in warm water.

The pug's dish was placed in front of him and he began to devour the food almost without moving.

Miss Jensen had lit a single candle. She drank her tea and ate rye bread and butter—sliced into neat little squares with her knife.

After she had drunk her tea, Miss Jensen went to bed. She carried the pug in her arms and put him at the foot of her comforter. Then she got the school ledger and placed it on the table next to her bed.

She locked the door and looked in all the corners and under the bed with her candle.

Then she undressed and combed out her braids and hung them up on the mirror.

The pug was already asleep and snoring on the comforter.

Miss Jensen had not slept well since Pastor Linde had said—those words.

Mrs. Bai walked along the road to the station. She opened the gate and went out on the platform. It was completely empty, so quiet that you could hear the humming of the two telegraph wires.

Mrs. Bai sat down on the bench outside the door with her hands in her lap and gazed out over the fields. She had a tendency to remain sitting that way, wherever there was a chair or a bench or a step.

She gazed out over the fields, the great expanses of plowed earth, and, farther off, the meadows. The sky was vast and bright blue. There was no resting place for the eyes at all, except for the church. With its stepped gables and its tower it was visible at the far edge of the flat field.

Mrs. Bai was cold; she stood up. She went over to the garden hedge and looked over it, opened the gate, and went in. The garden was a triangular strip along the track; in front was the vegetable garden, and in the farthest point was a lawn with some long-stemmed roses in front of a gazebo beneath an elder tree.

She examined the roses; there were still a few buds. They had certainly bloomed faithfully this year, and continuously.

But soon they would have to be covered up.

Look how the petals were already falling. But there was no shelter for anything, of course.

Mrs. Bai walked out of the garden and along the platform into the little courtyard behind the fence. She called the maid; she wanted to give some grain to the doves.

She received the grain in an earthenware bowl, and she began calling the doves and scattering the grain on the cobblestones.

She was so fond of doves. She had loved them ever since she was a child.

The large courtyard at her home in town had been so full of them. How they had hovered around the dovecote right across from the doorway to the workshop . . .

It was as if she could hear cooing and murmuring just by thinking of the courtyard back home.

The *old* courtyard—for later, after her father died, they had sold the workshop and everything and moved away.

The doves fluttered around Mrs. Bai and pecked at the grain.

"Marie," said Mrs. Bai, "look how peevish the spotted one is."

Marie stepped into the kitchen doorway and talked about the doves. Mrs. Bai emptied the bowl. "A few of them will have to be killed for Bai's *l'ombre* game," she said.

She went up the steps. "How early it gets dark now," she said and went inside.

In the parlor it was dimly lit and warm when she came in from outside. Mrs. Bai sat down at the piano and played.

She would only play at dusk, always the same three or four melodies, sentimental tunes which she played slowly and languidly, with exactly the same interpretation, so that they all came to sound alike.

Whenever she sat and played in the dark parlor, Mrs. Bai would almost always think about her home. There had been many brothers and sisters, and there was always so much activity back home.

She was the youngest of them all. While her father was still alive, she was so small that at dinner she could barely reach up to her plate.

Her father would sit on the sofa in his shirtsleeves and they would stand around the table, all the children, and reach for the food.

"Straighten up, children," said her father.

He sat there lolling with his broad back and his arms stretched out on the table.

Her mother went back and forth, fetching and carrying things.

Out in the kitchen all the boys from the workshop ate at the long table.

They snorted and argued so you could hear them through the door, and suddenly they would start such a fight that it seemed the house was going to collapse.

"What are you roughhousing about?" her father would shout and pound the table in the parlor.

Out in the kitchen it would become very still—with only the quiet rummaging of someone who was looking for something under the table after the skirmish.

"Those rascals," her father would say.

After dinner he slept on the sofa for an hour. He always woke up right on the dot.

"Well, I suppose I've thought enough about what's best for the country," he said and had coffee before he went out to the workshop.

When her father died, everything changed, of course. Katinka went to school with Consul Lassen's children and the mayor's Fanny.

And she was also invited to the consul's house.

The other brothers and sisters all left home. She was alone with her mother.

Those were Katinka's best years, there in that little town where she knew everyone and everyone knew her. In the afternoon she and her mother would sit in the parlor, each at her own place on the dais beneath the windows, and her mother had the window with the gossip mirror; Katinka did French embroidery or read.

The sun fell in bright stripes through the flowers in the windows, out across the white floor.

Katinka read many novels from the lending library about refined people, and poetry too, which she copied into a little album.

"Tinka," said her mother, "here comes Ida Levy. Oh, she's wearing that yellow hat."

Tinka looked up. "She's going to her music lessons," she said.

Ida Levy walked past, and there was a glance and a nod in reply and a gesture inquiring whether they were coming to meet "the 9:30" . . .

"It's shocking the way Ida Levy walks so crooked on her heels," said Tinka; she gazed after her.

"She gets that from her mother," said Katinka's mother.

One by one they walk past, the freight agent and the two lieutenants and the head clerk and the doctor. And they say hello, and up there they nod and say a few words about each one of them.

They know where each one is going and what he is going to do there.

They know every outfit and every flower on the hats. And every day they make the same comments about the same things.

Minna Helms goes past and nods.

"Did you see Minna Helms?" asks her mother.

"Yes." And Katinka stares after her and squints toward the sun. "She could use a new coat pretty soon."

"Poor things—where are they going to get that from?" Her mother looks in the mirror. "Yes—it does look shabby," she says. "I'd think they could put a border on it. But it's just like Mrs. Noes says—Mrs. Helms has so little, and she takes so little care of it."

"If only the head clerk would make good his intentions," said Tinka.

It was five o'clock and the young girls went to meet their girlfriends, and arm in arm they walked up and down the street, stopping to gather in groups and laugh and talk, and then they parted.

But in the evening, after tea, the mothers went along to the 9:30 train, and things were quieter along the road to the station.

"Katinka," said her mother, turning around (she was walking ahead with Mrs. Levy), "Mr. Bai... So he's off tonight..."

Mr. Bai came past and greeted them. And Katinka nodded and blushed. Her girlfriends were always teasing her about Mr. Bai.

"So he's going in to play ninepins," said Mrs. Levy.

On Sunday they went to the morning service. They were all dressed in their finery, and they sang so that it resounded beneath the vaulted ceiling as the sun came in through the big chancel windows.

It was so awful to sit next to Thora Berg in church.

The whole time the pastor was in the pulpit she would sit there and say: "All right, old man," and pinch her arm.

Yes, Thora Berg was always stirring up mischief.

In the evening, dirt and gravel would rain against Tinka's windowpanes.

And they would hear laughter and a commotion down the whole street.

"It's Thora coming home from a party," said Tinka. "They've been at the mayor's."

Thora set out for home down the street as if it were a wild chase, followed by all the young men. The whole town got to listen when Thora Berg went home from a party.

Katinka liked Thora Berg the best. She admired her and always watched her closely whenever they were together. Twenty times a day she would say at home, "That's what Thora said..."

They didn't really spend a lot of time together. But in the afternoon when they promenaded, or out at the pavilion for the subscription series—at concerts when the military played every other Wednesday—they would talk. Tinka would always blush whenever they met.

It was also at the pavilion that she had met Bai for the first time. On that very first evening he had danced with her the most.

And when they went skating he would always ask her to skate with him. It was as if they were flying, and almost as if he were carrying her. And he also visited her at home.

All her girlfriends teased her, and she always got him when they "wrote messages" and played "One Went Out" and when they "thought about something." It was always Bai, and then they would all laugh.

And at home her mother was always talking about him.

Then came the engagement period, and she always had someone to accompany her: to church on Sunday, and to the theater in winter, whenever there were actors in town. And after Bai got his position, there was the busy time with her trousseau and furnishings and all those things. Her girlfriends helped her with all the names that had to be stitched and everything that had to be hemmed.

They were summer days, and they all sat up in the gazebo together. The sewing machine whirred, making hems and stitching the seams.

And they teased her and laughed, and suddenly they would jump up and fly out into the garden and run around the lawn with noise and laughter, wild as a bunch of fillies.

Tinka was the quietest of them all.

There was whispering with girlfriends in all the corners and sewing get-togethers at the Levys', where they stitched the rug that Tinka was to stand on before the altar to be married—and they practiced the hymns they were going to sing in the choir.

Then the day came, and the wedding in the decorated church—it was so crowded, row after row. Up by the organ stood all the young girls. Tinka nodded to them and thanked them and wept again. She wept like a faucet the whole time.

And then they came out here to the silence.

In the beginning of her marriage, Tinka was scared and always anxious, as if someone were going to assault her.

There was so much she hadn't imagined, and Bai was so crude about so many things, which she mostly just suffered and endured, frightened and uncertain as she was.

She was also such a stranger and didn't know anyone at all.

Later there came a time when she was more amenable, mostly lazily acquiescent, as was her nature.

She would sit with her husband in his office with her crocheting, and she would look at him as he sat bent over his desk. Her curly hair fell slightly over her forehead.

She got up and went over to him and put her arm around his neck, and she would have liked to stay there like that, quietly—stay near him for a long time.

"My dear, I'm trying to write," said Bai.

She bent her neck to his mouth and he kissed it.

"May I write now?" he said, kissing her one more time.

"Writing fool," she said and left him.

The year passed. Katinka slipped into life with the trains that came and went, and the people of the region who went on trips and came back home; and they brought news and asked about news.

They got together with the people of the district. Mostly Bai's *l'ombre* games, to which the wives were invited every other time.

Then there was the dog and the doves and the garden. And Mrs. Bai was not the industrious type either. She never accomplished so much that time seemed to drag for her. She spent a long time on every single thing; Bai called her "Do It Tomorrow."

Children, however, they did not have.

When Katinka's mother died they received her inheritance. For two people they were well-to-do and had an abundance of everything.

Bai liked to eat well, and from Aalborg he took good wine and a great deal of it. He put on weight, and he went around in his indolence while his assistant did most of the work. He only played "the Lieutenant" outdoors.

He had a child up in the village.

"Damn it all," he said to Kiær, who was a bachelor, "a man *is* an old cavalry officer, after all. And the girl was as cute as a baby sparrow..."

The girl was sent to Aalborg after the damage was done. The child stayed up in the village, where it was being looked after.

That's the way time passed.

Katinka didn't read anymore, the way she did as a young girl. Books were just pretend, after all.

In her desk Mrs. Bai had a large cardboard box with many withered flowers, little ribbons, and frilly things made of tulle with inscriptions in gold-foil letters. They were her old cotillion mementos from the club and the "last subscription" at the pavilion when dances were held there.

She often took everything out on winter evenings and rearranged them all over again and tried to remember who had given her this one or that.

She would figure it all out and write the gentleman's name on the back of each cotillion card.

Bai sat drinking his toddy at the table.

"That old junk," he said.

"Leave it alone, Bai," she said. "Now that I've just arranged it all."

And she kept on writing her gentlemen's names.

Sometimes she would also read the verses that she had once copied into her old poetry album.

In the top drawer of her desk, under the silver chest, lay her bridal veil and the withered wreath of myrtle.

She would also pick them up and smooth them out and put them back again.

And she could sit for half an hour at a time in front of the open drawer not doing a thing, as was her custom.

Once in a while she would just smooth out the veil with her hands.

It had begun to turn quite yellow, her bridal veil.

But time was passing too. It was already ten years ago.

Yes—she would soon be an old woman. She had turned thirty-two.

The Bais were well liked in the area. Known as decent and hospitable people, where the coffeepot was immediately put on the stove as soon as an acquaintance appeared at the station.

Bai was a good man at a party; and at the station everything was in order, even though he himself might not be terribly enthusiastic on the job.

Mrs. Bai was rather quiet, but it was always pleasant to see her gentle face. She looked like a young girl when she sat among the wives at the big *l'ombre* parties.

"But there ought to be a couple of children," said Mrs. Linde when she trudged home in the evening from the Bais' house with the pastor. "Those well-to-do people—who could afford it. It's such a shame for them to sit there all alone . . ."

"God gives life according to His will, my dear," said the pastor.

"Yes, God's will be done," said his wife.

The pastor and his wife had had ten children.

Seven of them the Lord had taken as babies.

The old pastor remembered the seven whenever there were children to be buried in the parish.

Mrs. Bai had stopped playing. She was sitting there thinking that she really ought to get up and light the lamp. But then
she called for the maid to light it and remained seated.

Marie came in with the lamp. She put on the tablecloth and
set the table for tea.

"What time is it?" asked Mrs. Bai.

"The eight o'clock train was announced," said Marie.

"I didn't hear that at all . . ."

Mrs. Bai put on a wrap and went out. "Is the train here?"
she said in the office.

"Any minute," said Bai. He was standing by the telegraph
table.

"Is there a wire?"

"Yes."

"For whom?"

"Oh, up in the village . . ."

"Then Ane will have to go . . ."

Mrs. Bai went out onto the platform. She was so fond of
watching the train coming and going in the dark.

The sound, at first a long way off, and then the thundering
as the train went over the river bridge, and the great light that
raced forward, and finally the heavy, shuddering mass that
wound its way out of the night and became the individual
cars, stopping right in front of her with the conductors and
the illuminated mail car and the compartments . . .

Then, when it had left again and the roaring had died out,
everything lay quiet, almost doubly silent.

The station hand put out the lanterns, first the one on the
platform, then the one over the door.

There was nothing but the light from the two windows,
two little bridges of light out into the vast darkness.

Mrs. Bai went inside.

They drank tea, and afterwards Bai read the papers with a
toddy or two. Bai only read the Government press. He himself

took *The National Times*, and he read Kiær's *Daily*, which he took out of the mail bag.

He pounded the table so the toddy glass clattered whenever the opposition got "a great rap on the snout." And sometimes he would read individual sentences aloud and laugh.

Mrs. Bai listened quietly; she wasn't interested in politics. And there was a period when she was very sleepy in the evening as well.

"Well, I suppose it's about time," said Bai.

He got up and lit a lantern. He went his rounds to check that everything was shut and the track was set properly for the night train.

"You can go to bed, Marie," said Mrs. Bai out in the kitchen. She woke up Marie, who was asleep sitting up in the wooden chair.

"Good night, madam," she said sleepily.

"Good night."

Mrs. Bai moved the flowers in the parlor from the windowsill to the floor. That's where they stood at night in a row.

Bai came back.

"It's going to be cold tonight," he said.

"I thought so—because of the roses . . . I looked at them today."

"Yes," he said, "they'll have to be covered up now."

Bai began to undress in the bedroom. The door stood open.

He liked to walk back and forth for a long time in the evening. From the bedroom to the parlor in his underwear.

"That clumsy oaf," he said. Marie was thumping around loudly upstairs in the attic room.

Mrs. Bai placed white cloths over the furniture and locked the door to the office.

"Can I put it out?" she asked.

And she put out the lamp.

She came into the bedroom, sat down in front of the mirror, and unpinned her hair.

Bai was in his underpants and asked her for a scissors.

"Damn, you're getting thin," he said.

Katinka pulled her dressing gown around her.

Bai got into bed and lay there talking. She answered in her quiet way as usual; there was always just the slightest pause before her words came.

They were silent for a while.

"Hm, rather nice person—don't you think?"

"Yes—in appearance anyway . . ."

"What did Agnes Linde say?"

"Also that he was quite nice."

"Hm—sharp tongue that girl has. And the devil knows what kind of a *l'ombre* hand he plays . . ."

A little while later Bai was asleep,

When Bai slept, he breathed loudly through his nose.

Mrs. Bai was used to it by now.

She kept sitting in front of the mirror. She took off her dressing gown and looked at her neck.

Yes, she really had grown thin.

Ever since she had that cough in the spring.

Mrs. Bai put out the candles and lay down in the bed next to Mr. Bai.

Chapter Two

The days were short. The rain so torrential and the slush so thick. And constant gray skies and dampness. Even Miss Jensen's best pupils wore clogs across the fields to school.

At the station the platform was a lake. The last tiny leaves from the garden hedge came out to sail on it. The trains arrived dripping, the conductors ran around swathed in wet capes. Little Bentzen scurried along under an umbrella with the mail bags.

Kiær's grain wagons had oilcloth coverings, and the drivers sat in rain capes.

Foreman Huus drove the first wagon to the station himself. There was plenty to do with the freight and the paperwork.

"Here they come from Kiær's," called Bai to his wife.

Foreman Huus usually got out of his raincoat for half an hour and had a cup of coffee with the Bais.

While Mrs. Bai went back and forth setting the table for coffee, Huus and the farm hands would bustle around on the platform loading the sacks into the freight cars. Katinka saw them running past the windows. They looked so enormous in their oilskins.

The maid, Marie, was infatuated with Huus and always went around talking about him as she worked.

She never tired of praising his good points. And the last one was always: "And what a voice he has."

It was a soft, ingenuous voice, and no one knew exactly why Marie had fallen in love with it.

When Huus was finished outside they would come in for coffee. Inside it was warm and pleasant and there was a fragrance from a couple of potted plants still blooming on the windowsill.

"Yes—that's what I always say," said Huus, rubbing his hands. "It's nice at Mrs. Bai's house."

Huus brought a feeling of warmth with him too. There was a kind of quiet contentment about him; he was not a man of many words and he seldom told anecdotes. But he slipped so easily into the daily small talk, cheerful, always in a good humor. And people felt good just having him around.

A freight train arrived at that time, and Bai had to go out on the platform to attend to it.

It made no difference when he left and the other two remained alone. They chatted a little or were silent. She went over to the window and laughed at Bai, who was jumping around out there in the rain.

Huus looked at Katinka's flowers and gave her advice on how to take care of them. Katinka went over to him and they looked at the plants together. He knew every single one of them, whether it was putting out shoots or dormant, and what should be done with it.

Huus was interested in little things like that, in the doves and the new strawberry beds that had been put in that fall.

Katinka would ask his advice and they would walk around and look at one thing after another.

Bai had never cared for things like that. But with Huus it seemed that there was constantly something new to learn, to ask advice about, and to take care of.

So they always had plenty to talk about, in a quiet and sensible way, as was natural to both of them.

In fact, there was almost always something waiting for Huus—even though he came every day, as he did at this time because they were selling grain at Rugaard.

Miss Ida Abel often had errands at the station too. She

would make her way down the road with a letter that had to go with the morning mail.

"God, what weather, Lieutenant."

"A cup of coffee, Miss? A little internal fluid to give you strength? Huus is inside with my wife."

"Oh, are the men from Rugaard here?"

"Yes, with grain."

Little Ida had had no idea.

From the dais under the corner window of the farmhouse the "little chicks" had a panoramic view of the entire region.

Little Ida always sat there in the morning hours.

She began to take the curling papers out of her hair.

"Where are you going?" Big Louise was wearing a spice bag for her toothache.

"Taking letters to the station."

"Mother," whined Louise, "now Ida is running off again. Well, if you think you're going to have any luck there . . ."

"Is that any of your concern?" Little Ida slammed the bedroom door in her face.

"For God's sake, if you want to make yourself ridiculous—but take your own boots. I'm warning you, Ida . . . Mother, tell Ida she has to wear her own boots—she's always wearing my button shoes to the station."

"Oh pooh," says Ida, who is finished with the curling iron.

"And my gloves—*do* you mind . . ." Louise snatches a pair of gloves out of Ida's hands. And a couple of doors are slammed again.

"But what is it, children?" says Mrs. Abel. She comes in from the kitchen with her hands wet. She has been peeling potatoes.

"Ida is stealing my clothes." Miss Louise is crying with annoyance.

Widow Abel quietly picks up after Little Ida and goes back to her potatoes.

"Dear Mrs. Bai," said Little Ida in the doorway, "I won't come in. Hello, Mr. Huus, I look so awful . . . I'm just looking in. Good day."

Miss Abel came in. She was wearing a low-cut bodice under her raincoat.

"When Christmas draws near—everyone is so terribly busy. Oh, excuse me, Mr. Huus . . . I'd like to get by."

Miss Abel sat down on the sofa. "Lovely sitting here," she said.

But she didn't sit there for long. There were far too many things she had to admire. Miss Ida Abel was so youthfully ecstatic.

"Oh God, that little rug . . ."

Miss Abel just had to feel the little rug.

"Oh, Mr. Huus, pardon me . . ." She had to get by him again.

She felt the rug.

"Mother always says that I flutter about," said Little Ida.

Widow Abel occasionally called her daughters her "fluttering doves." But the name didn't stick. There was something about Big Louise that totally contradicted the term "dove."

And so they continued to be the "little chicks."

Whenever Miss Abel arrived, it wouldn't be long before Foreman Huus would leave.

"There isn't enough room in a parlor when Miss Ida is there," he said.

It was getting on toward Christmas.

Once a week Huus went to Randers on business. He

always had something to take care of for Mrs. Bai that Bai
mustn't hear about. The two of them would whisper together
in the parlor for a long time whenever Huus arrived on the
train.

Katinka thought it had been years since she had looked
forward to Christmas the way she was looking forward to it
now.

There was something in the air, too.

Bright, hard frost and snow covered the earth.

Whenever Huus had been to Randers, he would stay to tea
at the station. He came with the eight o'clock train. Mrs. Bai
would often still be sitting in the dusk.

"Would you play a little?" he asked.

"Oh, I only know a few . . ."

"But I'd still like to hear them." He sat down in a chair in
the corner next to the sofa.

Katinka played her five pieces that all sounded alike.
Normally she would never dream of playing for anyone. But
Huus sat so still over in his corner that she almost didn't
notice him. And besides, he was quite unmusical too.

After she had played, they might sit for a while without
saying anything, until Marie came in with the lamps and the
tea things.

After tea Bai took Huus into his office.

"Men have to be alone once in a while too," he said.

When they were alone, he and Huus, Bai would tell
wenching stories.

In his day he'd done plenty of it, too . . . when they were
in school.

"And Copenhagen had girls . . . Well—things aren't like
they used to be . . . They say they go to Russia now. Yes—that
might very well be. Aren't like they used to be . . . When
you've known Kamilla—Kamilla Andersen—nice girl—
splendid girl . . . Came to a bad end, that girl, damned if she
didn't throw herself out of a window . . . Ambitious girl."

Bai winked. Huus pretended that he understood Kamilla's ambition.

"Very ambitious girl . . . Knew her, splendid."

Bai talked the whole time. Huus smoked his cigar and didn't look particularly interested.

"And I ask them too, you know," said Bai, "the young people, during summer vacation, at the parsonage: 'What kind of girls do you have now?' I ask. 'Are they any good?' 'Little girls, old friend. Little girls.' Yes . . . they say they go to Russia—could very well be."

Huus expressed no opinion about where they went. He looked at the clock.

"I suppose it's about time," he said.

"Oh . . . well . . ."

But Huus had to go. "It's a forty-five-minute walk, you know."

They went in to Mrs. Bai.

"Why don't we keep Huus company," she said. "It's so lovely out."

"What the hell—stretch the legs a little."

They walked along with Huus.

Katinka walked with her arm in Bai's. Huus on the other side of her, the snow creaking under their feet along the road.

"Look how many stars there are this year," said Katinka.

"Yes, a lot more than last year, Tik." Bai was always lively after he had spent time alone.

"Yes, I think so too," said Katinka.

"Strange thing about the weather," said Huus.

"Yes"—that was Bai—"this cold spell before Christmas."

"And it'll last through New Year's . . ."

"You think so?"

Then they were silent, and when they spoke again, it was about something similar.

At the bend in the road the Bais said good night.

Mrs. Bai hummed along the way. When they got home she

stood in the doorway as Bai took the lantern and went over to check the track for the night train.

He came back. "Well . . ." he said.

Katinka breathed out into the air.

"How nice the cold is," she said, slicing through her own breath in the air with her hand.

They went inside.

Bai was lying in bed smoking the stub of a cigar. Then he said, "Yes—Huus is a damned nice fellow . . . But he's a stick-in-the-mud."

Mrs. Bai was sitting in front of the mirror. She laughed.

But Bai confided to Kiær that he'd be damned if Huus knew anything about women.

"I feel him out—you know," he said, "in the evening when he's visiting us. But I'll be damned if he knows much about women . . ."

"So, old Bai," said Kiær, and they slapped each other on the back and laughed heartily. "Not everyone can be a connoisseur."

"No—fortunately. And Huus—I'll be damned if—"

They were called in to coffee.

It was a busy time at the station during the last days before Christmas. Things were picked up and dropped off. No one wanted to wait for the mailman.

The Misses Abel sent little cards with Christmas wishes and inquired about packages.

Miss Jensen brought a cigar box; she had used a whole stick of sealing wax to decorate the twine all the way around.

"My own handiwork, Mrs. Bai," said Miss Jensen. The handiwork was for her sister.

Mrs. Bai said, "Mrs. Abel was in Randers yesterday, you know."

"Her semi-annual payment has come in," said Miss Jensen caustically.

"She was so weighted down when she came home."

"I believe it."

"You're going to the Abels' on Christmas Eve?"

"No . . . we live right next door to each other, Mrs. Bai. But the Abels . . . always have enough to do remembering each other. In the past I've always gone over to the Lindes', at the parsonage. No, the Abels," said Miss Jensen, "oh, no—not everyone is alike . . ."

Mrs. Bai asked Miss Jensen if she would perhaps like to come to their house.

She managed to tell Bai in the evening when he came in from the track.

"Mathias," she said (she used Mathias for her more dubious announcements), "I had to ask Miss Jensen over for Christmas Eve. She can't go over to the Lindes'."

"Well, I don't care"—Bai hated "that little wig stand"— "as long as *you* take care of the soup kitchen."

Bai walked around a bit.

"Isn't she going to the Abels'?" he said.

"That's just it—they haven't invited her, Mathias."

"Well—that was a damned good decision," said Bai, who was pulling off his boots. "Well, it's up to you."

Mrs. Bai was glad that she had managed to tell him.

Miss Jensen arrived at 5:30 with a basket and the pug.

She made excuses for Bel-Ami.

"He's usually over at the Abels'—I usually take him over to the Abels'. But tonight, you understand, I didn't feel . . . but he won't make any trouble . . . he's a quiet animal."

Bel-Ami was settled on a rug in the bedroom. There he stayed. He suffered from sleeping sickness and was no bother except that he snored.

"He sleeps because of a good heart," said Miss Jensen, taking her collar and cuffs out of the basket.

Bel-Ami was only difficult when he was supposed to go home. He had totally lost his taste for movement.

Every ten steps he would stop and howl with his tail between his legs.

When no one was looking, Miss Jensen would pick him up and carry Bel-Ami in her arms.

They ate at six o'clock. The tree stood in the corner. Little Bentzen was there with brushed pompadour, wearing his confirmation suit.

He ate like a wolf.

Bai constantly refilled the glasses and touched Miss Jensen's and Bentzen's goblets with his own.

"So, *skaal*, Miss Jensen. *Skaal*, my good Bentzen—it's only Christmas once a year," he said. He kept on filling their glasses.

Little Bentzen's face was turning as red as a lobster.

"We're drinking just like they did in the heathen days," said Miss Jensen.

The door stood open to the office. The telegraph tapped incessantly.

The colleagues were wishing each other "Merry Christmas" along the line. Bai went back and forth to reply.

"Say hello from me," said Katinka.

"Merry Christmas from Mundstrup," said Bai from the apparatus.

"Yes," said Miss Jensen, "that's what I tell my pupils; our age has dissolved the bounds of space, I always say."

By the time they got to the apple fritters, Miss Jensen had grown lively. She nodded childishly to herself in the mirror and said *skaal*.

Miss Jensen was wearing a new chignon that she had given herself for Christmas. She was now wearing three different shades of hair.

Little by little Miss Jensen grew quite pleased with herself.

After dinner, while the tree was being lit, Little Bentzen tried to play leapfrog with Marie out in the kitchen.

Katinka moved about quietly, taking her time lighting the tree. She also wanted to be alone for a while.

"God knows whether Huus has gotten our package," she said. She was standing on a chair and lighting the candles with a wax taper.

At the last moment she took a scarf from a table—her sister had sent it to her—and put it at Miss Jensen's place. There were so few gifts at her place; she was sharing the sofa with Little Bentzen.

Katinka opened the door to the office, and they all came in for the tree.

They walked around looking at their things, thanking each other, half embarrassed. Miss Jensen got little tissue-paper packages out of her basket and took them around to their places.

Marie came in wearing a white apron. She went around with her own presents in her arms, feeling the corners of the objects.

The eight o'clock train was attended to, and they sat once more in the parlor. The tree was still lit in its corner.

It was quite warm and smoky in there from all the candles on the tree.

Bai, halfheartedly fighting off sleep, said, "All this celebrating is exhausting, Miss Jensen. All this Christmas cheer fills you up."

They were all sleepy and looked at the clock. The two women kept talking about the presents and how they were made.

"I think I'll go in and see how the world is being governed," said Bai. He escaped to the office. Little Bentzen was sitting asleep in a chair under the pipe rack.

The two women were alone. They sat in a corner near the piano, in front of the tree, and felt very sleepy.

They dozed off for a moment, and both jumped in fright at

a crackling sound from the tree. One of the branches had caught fire.

"It's almost burned out," said Katinka, putting out the fire.

The candles began to burn out one by one, and the tree grew dark. They sat there, wide awake again, and gazed at the darkened tree—only a couple of candles still flickered.

They were both seized with the same quiet melancholy as they looked at the last tiny lights; they only seemed to empha-size the dark, dead tree.

Miss Jensen began to talk. At first Katinka hardly listened to what she was saying; she was lost in her own thoughts about her family back home and about Huus.

Katinka didn't know why she had been thinking so much about Huus all evening. He had been in her thoughts the whole time.

The whole time...

She nodded to Miss Jensen and pretended to be listening.

Miss Jensen was talking about her youth, and suddenly she started to tell her love story. She was already in the midst of the tale when Katinka became aware of it and wondered why Miss Jensen happened to be talking about that now, and to her...

It was quite a simple story about a love that had not been returned. She had thought the love was for her, but it was for her girlfriend.

Miss Jensen spoke softly, in an even, subdued voice; she had her handkerchief out, and once in a while she would dab her cheeks and sniff a little.

Katinka slowly began to feel moved. Then she thought about how that little wrinkled woman must have looked when she was young. Perhaps she had had a trim little figure after all.

And now here she sat, forsaken and alone.

Katinka was touched to the heart, and she took Miss Jensen's hands and patted them gently.

The old woman wept even harder at her caress. Katinka kept on patting her hands.

The last stumps of candles burned out, and the Christmas tree stood completely dark.

"And a single woman has to make it through life," said Miss Jensen, "no matter what traps they might set at her feet."

Miss Jensen had once again come around to the pastor and his "words."

Katinka let go of Miss Jensen's hand. She thought the room had grown quite cold and unpleasant around the dark tree.

Bai threw open the door of the bright office. A messenger had come riding with a package from Huus.

"The lamps, Marie," called Katinka, running into the office with the package.

It was a very fine net shawl shot through with golden threads, a large one that could be folded up into nothing.

Katinka kept standing there with the shawl. It made her so happy. She had had a quite similar one, but only a few weeks ago it had been singed and ruined.

But this one was much finer.

And she kept on standing there with the shawl.

Now Bai was cheerful again; he had slept off his dinner, and they all drank a couple of shots of the genuine rum in their tea.

Little Bentzen grew so merry that he ran across to his room and got some poems that he had written on many scraps of paper, on the backs of old tariffs and invoices.

He read aloud, and Bai slapped his belly with laughter. Katinka sat there smiling with Huus's fine shawl wrapped around her.

Finally Miss Jensen played a Tyrolean waltz, and Little Bentzen, rather embarrassed, flew out into the kitchen and waltzed with Marie, making her shriek.

They all had to help wake up Bel-Ami when it was time for

Miss Jensen to go; he absolutely refused to leave his rug. Bai stepped on his stump of a tail when Miss Jensen wasn't looking.

Little Bentzen was to escort her home. But Miss Jensen, who was as scared of the dark as a rabbit, wanted to go alone.

Miss Jensen refused to carry Bel-Ami whenever anyone was watching.

They all followed her out to the platform gate and shouted "Merry Christmas! Merry Christmas!" over the hedge.

Bel-Ami howled in the middle of the snow-covered road. He refused to budge.

When Miss Jensen saw that they had all gone inside, she bent down and lifted Bel-Ami under her arm.

Miss Jensen was bundled up like an Eskimo woman as she walked home on Christmas Eve.

Katinka threw open the windows in the parlor so that the biting air came in.

"Hm, that little pretender," said Bai. He was quite benevolently pleased with little Miss Jensen's visit that evening.

"The poor thing," said Katinka. She kept standing at the window, gazing out across the white field in the night.

"You wouldn't think you'd been complaining about a cough," said Bai. He closed the door to the bedroom.

Bentzen walked across the platform to his room.

"She was carrying the pug," he said. He had hidden behind the hedge in order to observe the event. "Merry Christmas, ma'am."

"Merry Christmas, Bentzen."

A few doors closed, and then it was totally silent.

There was only the delicate humming of the telegraph wires now and then.

Katinka was outside feeding the doves before they went to church. The air was clear and still, and the bells were ringing down past the woods. Scattered across the white fields you could see the farmers trudging in single file along the shoveled pathways on their way to the offertory.

They were waiting in a crowd outside the church, wishing each other "Merry Christmas." The women held out their fingertips to each other and whispered.

Then they stood still, looking at each other, until someone new joined the circle.

The Bais arrived rather late, and the church was full. Katinka nodded "Merry Christmas" to Huus, who was standing right near the door, and walked up to her place.

She shared a pew with the Abels, right behind the pastor's family.

The little Abel "chicks" had disappeared behind their veils and fantastic wrappings.

Mrs. Linde had eyes in the back of her head on the great offering days. She "dressed" herself and her daughter for the offering days and the fatted calves.

Miss Linde never went to church when there was the "waltz of the offering plate in the chancel."

They sang the old Christmas hymns, which gradually won them all over, both young and old. They sounded so strong and joyous beneath the vaulted ceiling. The winter sun streamed in brightly through the windows onto the white walls. With humble, quiet words old Linde spoke about the shepherds in the field and the people for whom that day a savior was born, words which descended like the peace of simplicity over his church.

The Christmas spirit came over Katinka as the offering procession went up around the altar in a long line. The men walked stiffly, thudding on the tiles, and returned to their places with no change in expression.

The women shuffled along, embarrassed and red in the face, staring intently at their folded handkerchiefs.

Mrs. Linde had her eyes on the people's *hands* at the altar.

Mrs. Linde had been a pastor's wife for thirty-five years

and had sat through countless offerings. She could tell from the hands how much each person gave.

The hands moved out of the pockets differently when they gave a little than when they gave a lot.

Mrs. Linde estimated the offering to be average.

Outside the church the Bais met Huus. People were taking deep breaths of the fresh air and there was a great deal of wishing "Merry Christmas" again.

The pastor came with the offerings in a tied-up handkerchief and everyone greeted him and curtsied. "So, Miss Jensen, I suppose we should wish each other 'Merry Christmas,' " said the old pastor.

Katinka went out through the gate with Huus. Bai stayed a little behind with Kiær, so the two of them walked along the road alone.

The sun was lower over the brightly glittering fields; here and there some of the farms had the flag raised on flagpoles in the clear air.

All around, the church guests were going home in groups.

Katinka still had the Christmas hymns in her ears; she felt everything with a sense of joyous celebration.

"Christmas is lovely," she said.

"Yes," he said, putting all his conviction into that "yes."

"And he spoke so beautifully too," he added after a moment.

"Yes," said Katinka, "it was quite a beautiful sermon."

They walked on for a while.

"But I haven't even thanked you for the shawl," Katinka said then.

"Oh, don't mention it."

"Oh yes . . . it made me so happy. I had one almost like it, but it was singed."

"Yes, I know. You were wearing that shawl on the day I arrived."

Katinka wanted to say: How did you know that? But did not say it. She didn't know why she suddenly blushed, either, and for the first time she noticed that they weren't saying anything, and she searched for something to break the silence with.

They had reached the woods, and the church bells were chiming. It seemed as though the bells would never stop ringing that day.

"You'll come in, won't you?" said Katinka. "So you don't carry Christmas away with you."

They stood on the platform and listened to the bells as they waited for Bai.

Huus stayed the whole day.

When Bai sat down at the table, which shone with its damask tablecloth and many glass plates, he said: "Yes, it's good to be home with your family."

Little Bentzen shouted, "Yes, sir," and laughed with glee.

Huus didn't say a word. He just sat there, as Katinka said, and his eyes were happy.

And all day a quiet joy rested over the house.

In the evening they played whist. Little Bentzen made up a fourth.

In the parsonage they were counting the offerings wrapped in the pieces of paper. Mrs. Linde was disappointed. The offering was significantly less than in an average year.

"Why is that, Linde?" she asked.

The pastor sat thoughtfully looking at the many *small* coins.

"Why? These people think we can live like the lilies of the field."

Mrs. Linde pauses and for the last time counts the one-krone pieces.

"And with a family," adds Mrs. Linde.

"Well, my dear," says old Linde, "at least let's be grateful for the tithes."

The pastor's daughter and Curate Andersen were amusing themselves by overturning the furniture in the parlor; they were playing croquet.

"I'm hiding from Mother," said Miss Agnes. "All of Mother's less noble elements are stirred up on the great offering days."

Christmas was over.

Katinka thought that she hadn't had such a nice, homey Christmas for a long time, not since she was back home. Not that there was anything more special than usual; they went over to the Lindes' with Huus and a few others, and Miss Linde and the curate came over one evening with Kiær and Huus. The Misses Abel were there for the afternoon train and were invited in too. And after the eight o'clock train, they danced in the waiting room and sang along.

It was nothing special. But everything seemed to be so pleasant.

The only one who was "fretting" a little was Huus. He was constantly falling into a reverie lately.

"Huus," Katinka would say, "are you asleep?"

Huus would give a start as he sat there.

Bai was quite overcome by the comfortable atmosphere in the house.

"Hell of a difference the weather can make," he said as he stood out on the platform after attending to the afternoon train. "Damned if I don't feel surprisingly good lately— surprisingly good."

And during this period their whole marriage seemed shifted and moved years back in time. Not in any passionate or intense way, but intimately and pleasantly.

It was New Year's Eve, close to midnight. The Bais were still up in order to drink a toast to the new year.

There was a loud racket against the fence.

"What the devil?" exclaimed Bai; it startled both him and Bentzen, who were playing "sixty-six." "You'd think Peter could cut back on the ammunition a little."

There was a knocking on the window and Huus's voice shouted, "Happy New Year!"

"What the hell—is that Huus?" said Bai, getting up.

"That's what I thought," said Katinka. The commotion had made her heart pound.

Bai went out and opened the door. Huus was in a sleigh.

"For God's sake," said Bai, "come inside and have a drink."

"Good evening, Huus." Katinka appeared in the doorway. "We're drinking a toast to the new year," she said.

They tied up the horse in the storehouse and Katinka gave it some bread.

They drank a toast to the new year and decided to stay up for the night train. It came past at two a.m.

"Play us a tune, Tik," said Bai.

Katinka played a polka and Bai hummed along.

"Yes," he said, "I was a great dancer in my day, wasn't I, Tik?" He tickled her on the throat.

They went out onto the platform. The sky was overcast for the first time in a long while.

"More snow coming," said Bai. He grabbed some powdery snow and tossed it in Little Bentzen's face. There was quite a skirmish for a while.

"*There* it is," said Bai. They heard the train like a distant roar. "Damned dark tonight."

The noise came closer. Now the locomotive was clattering across the bridge. The little light was coming nearer and getting bigger; then the locomotive burst out of the darkness like a great, bright-eyed beast.

All four of them stood still as it rattled quickly past. It left steam in its wake, and light from the cars fell over the snow.

It moved on, rumbling into the darkness.

"Hm," said Katinka, "so that's the way we go into the new year." They had been standing in silence.

She leaned against her husband and rubbed her hair against his cheek.

Bai was also moved by the moment. He bent down and kissed her.

The train was roaring in the distance. They all turned and went inside.

Huus took out his anger on the horse as he drove home in the sleigh. He gave the horse the whip so it took off, and curses too.

It was dark, and a storm was brewing.

Katinka couldn't sleep. She woke up Bai.

"Bai," she said.

"What is it?" Bai turned over.

"It's such terrible weather..."

"Well, we're not out on the sea, at least," said Bai; he was half asleep.

"But there's a blizzard," said Katinka. "Do you think Huus is home by now, Bai?"

"Oh, for God's sake..."

Bai went back to sleep.

But Katinka couldn't sleep. She was afraid for Huus, who was out on the road in that weather. It was so dark—and he was new to the area.

How strange it was to realize that it was only three months ago that Huus had come here.

Was he home yet? Katinka listened again to the storm, which was getting worse. And he had been so sad tonight too—sitting by himself—she knew him well—and looking so miserable. There must be something wrong.

There *had* been something wrong lately...

If only he were home by now—the storm was growing.

Katinka dozed off and slept beside her husband.

The day after New Year's Day there was a party at the parsonage.

Half the district came, and there was talking and chattering throughout the house and all the way out to the hallway. It was always like that: people's tongues were loosened when they came to the parsonage.

The Abel family didn't arrive until they had started to play the proverb game. They always arrived late.

"Time always runs away from us," said Mrs. Abel. "We can never tear ourselves loose from the nest."

Whenever the Misses Abel were going out, they would walk around in their dressing gowns after dinner and quarrel. Mrs. Abel had to get dressed at the last minute and always looked as if a storm had ravaged her.

They played the proverb game so that not a stitch was left hanging in any wardrobe in the parsonage.

Miss Agnes played a fat man dressed in farmer's pants, and after that a Greenlander, with Katinka as the Greenlander's wife.

"Lovely woman," she said, "you're no prude."

They danced the *pingasut* until Katinka was quite dizzy. Mrs. Bai was so happy that she was almost giddy.

Little Ida was in charge of the other team. It mostly had something to do with a harem or a large spa. Whatever it was, Little Ida was embraced and hugged by a threadbare, blond second lieutenant.

The older people crowded into the doorways to watch. Outside the bay windows in the garden stood the farm hands, the two farmers, and the servants laughing at their "clever" young mistress.

Old Pastor Linde walked back and forth. "They're having fun, they're having fun," he said and went over to the older people.

Widow Abel gazed after the pastor; she was sitting next to the miller's wife.

"Yes, it certainly is lively here."

"Yes," said the miller's wife. "A lively pastor's house." Her tone was a little stern on the word "pastor."

Her daughter Helene was standing by her side. She preferred not to take part in the game.

The miller had built a new farmhouse and wanted to move up in society. They gave two parties a year where people sat in a circle and stared at the new furniture. Everything was always new.

All the furniture was covered with handicraft pieces that Miss Helene had made.

Ordinarily the family used a parlor in "the old wing." Once a week a fire was made in the new farmhouse so that the furniture wouldn't be damaged.

Miss Helene was an only child. She had been taught by Miss Jensen, with special attention to instruction in foreign languages. She was the most elegant lady in the region, with a particular taste for gold ornaments. No matter what her dress, she always wore gray felt shoes and white cotton stockings indoors.

In the company of others she was easily offended, and she would take her place at her mother's side with a frown on her face.

"Yes," says Mrs. Abel, "my little chicks sometimes find it a little too lively..."

"Mother," says Little Ida, "give me your handkerchief."

"Of course." Little Ida grabs it rather roughly from the widow.

Little Ida is supposed to dress up in a nightcap but finds that her own handkerchief is rather soiled.

"They're so excited with their game," says Mrs. Abel to the miller's wife.

The proverb game is over, and they play a quick blind-man's buff before dinner. There is shrieking in the parlor and such a commotion that the old wood stove bends before it.

"The wood stove," they shriek, "the wood stove!"

"Back, back."

Little Ida is so exhausted that she swoons. She can't breathe because her heart is pounding so hard. "Feel this," she says, placing the lieutenant's hand on her breast. "Feel how my heart is pounding."

Katinka is the blindman and is twirled around so she can barely stand.

"Oh, just look at the lovely woman," shouts Miss Agnes.

"Back, back."

Katinka captures Huus.

"Who's that?"

He bends down, and Katinka touches his hair. "It's Huus," she shouts. Old Pastor Linde claps his hands, signaling that dinner is served.

"Huus," says Katinka, "what's wrong? There *is* something the matter with you, isn't there?"

"Why do you think that?"

"You don't seem very happy lately... not like before."

"There's nothing wrong, Mrs. Bai."

"And I'm so happy now," says Katinka.

"Yes," says Huus, "that's quite obvious."

Bai came in from the card game. "Lord, how you look," he said.

Katinka laughed. "Yes, we've been doing a Greenland dance." She went into dinner with Huus.

Bai snatches Little Ida away from the lieutenant, who follows with the schoolmaster's son.

"Hansen," says the lieutenant, "who *is* that girl?"

"Oh, her mother, the one over there leaning on the pastor, lives here on the farm on a pension."

"A hell of a girl," says the lieutenant. "She has a damned nice figure."

Everyone takes a seat; the pastor sits at the head of the table. During the meal he proposes two toasts: "To those who are absent" and "To the spirit of good company." The same toasts have been proposed in the same words for seventeen years at that parsonage.

Finally they have marzipan cake with party snappers. The pastor pulls a snapper with Miss Jensen.

The lieutenant has wedged in a chair behind Little Ida. It's so cramped that she almost has to sit on his lap.

It's impossible to hear anything while they're laughing and pulling snappers and reading the fortunes out loud.

"Yes," says old Linde, "that's youth for you."

"Huus, it's our turn," says Katinka. She holds out a party snapper.

Huus pulls on it. "You got the fortune," says Katinka.

Huus reads what it says on the scrap of paper. "Stupid rubbish," he says, ripping it in two.

"But Huus, what did it say?"

"All bakery helpers write about love," says Little Ida across the table.

"Miss Ida"—that's the lieutenant—"shall we?"

Little Ida turns around again and pulls on a snapper with the lieutenant. "God, how unseemly," she yells. She gets a fortune about kissing, which the lieutenant reads aloud with his little handlebar mustache right up against her cheek.

The chairs are pushed back a little from the table, and the ladies fan themselves with the napkins. The young people are flushed with the heat and the milk punch, which is being passed around in big gray pitchers.

A pale little student gives a cheer for "Pastor Linde's patriarchal home," and everyone stands up and shouts "Hurrah!" The little student clinks glasses alone with the pastor.

"You little 'red' fellow," says old Linde, "are you drinking a toast to me?"

"One can have regard for *individuals,*" says the pale little man.

"Well, well," says old Linde, "well, well... Yes, youth has to have something to fight for, you see, Madam..."

Mrs. Abel is preoccupied with her Little Ida. She is so lively. She is practically lying in the lieutenant's arms.

"Yes, Your Reverence. Ida, my sweet girl"—my sweet girl doesn't hear her—"Little Ida, drink a glass with your mama," says Mrs. Abel.

"*Skaal,*" says Little Ida. "Lieutenant Nielsen," she hands him his glass, "drink with Mother."

Widow Abel smiles. "Oh—oh—what ideas my Little Ida has."

The pale little student inquires whether Miss Helene has read Schandorph.

Miss Helene reads books from the lending library.

"Schandorph has his merits—but he lacks a larger perspective." The little student feels obliged to say that Gjellerup is *his* writer.

Miss Helene cannot recall whether Mr. Gjellerup is included in the lending library.

"In him one finds the great ideas," the student continues, "knowledge combined with poetry. I would call him the most genuine fruit of our mighty Brandes... the freedom of the spirit."

"Brandes, isn't he that Jew?" says Miss Helene. No other impression of "freedom of the spirit" remains—at the miller's.

The student turns his enthusiasm to the great Darwin.

Bai has said something that has made Miss Jensen's face turn red.

"You're so awful," says Little Jensen, slapping him on the fingers.

"But Huus," says Katinka, "you have to take life as it comes ... and ..."

"And?"

"And actually it's all so wonderful ..."

"Lieutenant," shouts Miss Ida, "you're *hideous*."

Old Pastor Linde is sitting at the head of the table with his hands folded, nodding.

"Shall we thank Mother for the dinner?" he says, getting up.

Around the room there is a scraping of chairs and compliments on the dinner. In the parlor Agnes is already seated at the piano; it's time to dance.

"I don't know if you've seen *Ida*," says Big Louise to the widow. "She makes me feel like sinking into the ground."

Little Ida and the lieutenant are the first couple on the floor.

"Step lively," shouts Miss Agnes from the piano. She's playing "On My Settee" so the strings are jumping.

Bai dances with Katinka until they start making the rounds of the rooms; holding each other by the hands everyone whirls out through the doors.

Old Linde is in the lead with the gasping Miss Jensen.

"Linde, Linde," shouts Mrs. Linde, "your old legs!"

Miss Agnes pounds the keys like thunder.

"God—I'm dying," says Helene, the miller's daughter.

All of a sudden the chain breaks. Panting, the couples fall into chairs around the room.

"Phew, that made me hot," says Bai to the lieutenant and wipes his face. "Wonder if we could find a beer."

The lieutenant is amenable. They walk through the house. In the dining room the beers are standing on a windowsill.

"Is it local beer?" asks the lieutenant.

"No, it's Carlsberg."

"Then I'll have one."

"Here's a comfortable corner," said Bai. They went into

the pastor's study, a little room with the collected works of Oehlenschlæger and Mynster on the green-painted book-shelves and Thorvaldsen's bust of Christ over the desk.

They sat down with their beer at the table.

"Yes, I saw what was going on, all right," said Bai. "But I thought, let him have his fun, I thought—and her too . . ."

"Yes, a devil of a girl . . . she has a damned nice figure . . . and she's a splendid dancer, Stationmaster. Presses right up against you."

"Well, what the hell *can* she do, poor girl," said Bai, downing his beer.

"But what kind of girl is *she?*" asked the lieutenant. He meant Miss Agnes.

"Nice girl," said Bai. "No, there's nothing to be had there. Friend of my wife's."

"I see," said the lieutenant. "Yes, I thought so: a chatter-box—I know the kind."

The conversation turned to generalities. "These village girls—as a whole," said the lieutenant, "they're nice enough. I mean . . . but—you see, Stationmaster—no sophistication . . . No, the city, you know—that's something quite different."

The lieutenant had "discovered something."

"You see—we live in the neighborhood. That's where they put the castle—we *have* to live there . . . at one of the two pubs, either *Berren* or *Vesten.*"

"But are there any little girls?" asked Bai.

"Sassy little girls—damned sassy little girls."

"Well, I don't know . . . I'm a married man, after all, Lieu-tenant . . . It's window shopping, you understand, window shopping—even if you're over there for a couple of days . . . Window shopping," he repeated once again.

"Believe me—sassy girls," said the lieutenant, "sophisti-cated girls . . ."

"But they say they're going to Russia now."

"Yes, that's what they say."

Pastor Linde came in. "So here you are, Stationmaster," he said, walking across the room.

"Yes, Pastor—we're sitting here and philosophizing a bit—very quietly. With a stolen beer."

"Be my guest. Yes, it's nice in here." The pastor turned around in the doorway. "They're playing forfeits out there," he said.

Bai and the lieutenant went in to the forfeits game.

They were just about to fall into the well in there.

The little student with the most genuine fruit "fell" for Katinka.

"Kissing time!" shouted Miss Agnes.

Katinka turned her cheek so that "the fruit" could kiss her. He was red in the face and came closer to kissing her on the nose.

Katinka laughed and clapped her hands. "I'm falling, I'm falling..."

"For Huus," she said.

Huus came over and bent down. He kissed her hair.

"I'm falling for Miss Jensen," he said. His voice cracked as though he were hoarse.

Miss Jensen was still thinking about that kiss after she was home in bed with Bel-Ami.

Katinka consoled herself a little with the thought of the radical student.

The guests had left.

Miss Agnes was standing in the parlor looking around at the dance floor. Not one thing was in its proper place; glasses stood on the floor in the corners, and pudding dishes had been set down on the bookshelf.

"Ugh," she said, sitting down, "it looks like a certain man's foyer."

Curate Andersen had come in. "Well," she said, "yes—you have been rather nice tonight."

"Miss Agnes, does that amuse you?"

"No."

"Then why do you do it?"

"I'll tell you why, because it amuses the others. But you always have to be the one to make a fuss. Now give me a hand, so we can put some order into things." She started moving the furniture back into place.

"I'm not going out with Ida anymore, Mother," said Big Louise. "I won't, I tell you—it's scandalous for everyone."

"Because I just let you sit there? I'm supposed to keep you company, is that it?"

The widow never got involved in their quarrels. She knew they would keep at it while they put the curling papers in their hair. She went quietly about, putting away the clothing that belonged to the "little chicks."

"You get damned tired from all that celebrating," said Bai. He felt quite stiff in the legs as they walked.

Katinka didn't answer. Silently they walked home down the road.

Chapter Three

I t was springtime.
    In the afternoon the pastor's daughter would come to get Katinka, and they would walk down to the river. Little Bentzen had put a bench on the bank beneath a couple of willow trees close to the railroad bridge. There they sat and worked until the afternoon train arrived. The conductors on the line knew them and waved.

"The best thing would be to go away," said Agnes Linde, gazing after the train. "I think about it every day."

"Oh, but Agnes . . ."

"Yes, that would be the best—for the both of us—either he or I . . . should go away."

And for the thousandth time they would talk about that eternal topic.

It was a day in the middle of winter. Agnes Linde and the curate had come past on their way from the pond where they had been skating. The curate had to bring a letter over, and he fell into conversation with Bai.

Agnes came into the parlor with her skates over her arm. She was very brusque and said only "yes" and "no" in reply to Katinka's questions. Then she had stood at the window and looked out, and suddenly she began to cry.

"What is it, Miss Linde? Are you ill?" asked Katinka, going over and putting her arm around her. "What's the matter?"

Agnes Linde fought back her tears, but her sobs grew stronger and stronger. She pushed Katinka's arm away.

"Let me go in there," she said and went into the bedroom.

And there she threw herself onto the bed and told Katinka everything in one long stream: how she loved Andersen, and how he was just toying with her, and how she couldn't stand it anymore.

From that day on, Katinka had been Miss Linde's confidante.

Katinka was used to being confided in. It had always been like that at home too, when she was a girl. To her came all the wounded hearts. It was probably because of her quiet nature and because she herself never said very much. She was so well suited to listening to others.

The pastor's daughter came over almost every day, and she would stay with Katinka for hours. It was the same topic over and over again: her love and him. And every day she would describe what had been said thousands of times as if it were something new.

After she had been sitting and talking for three or four hours and had wound up crying in the end, Agnes would pack up her work.

"Well, we certainly are a couple of fine hens," she would say at last.

Now that spring had arrived, they sat down by the river.

Agnes would talk and Katinka would listen. She sat with her hands in her lap and looked out over the meadows. It was hazy out there, and the hollow resembled a great blue lake. You couldn't tell what was lake and what was sky; it was all just one hazy blue. With the clusters of willow bushes like islands in the sea.

Agnes told her about the first time, when she came home from Copenhagen and met Andersen. Months had passed, and she had no idea that she was fond of him.

Katinka listened and didn't listen. She knew the topic and she nodded quietly.

But gradually she became a participant in the strange love affair. She was familiar with all of its emotions. She shared them as if they were her own. Nothing else was ever discussed.

And all the words of love felt so familiar to her. Her thoughts became so intimate with everything that belonged to that love—of the two strangers.

After she accompanied Agnes Linde a way down the road and had turned back, she could sit for half an hour at a time in the gazebo beneath the elder in the garden. And all the words of love seemed to hover in the air around her, and she heard them again and pondered them.

It was part of her quiet, slightly indolent nature: words and thoughts she was preoccupied with would return to her again and again, along the road.

And they would *enmesh* her. And turn into dreams that led her far away, she scarcely knew where.

It had also been quieter at the Bais' lately. Huus didn't come to visit as often in the springtime. There was so much to do, he said.

When he did come, he was always in such an unpredictable mood. He often seemed not to notice at all how happy Katinka was to see him, and he talked mostly with Bai, even though Katinka had so much to tell him and to ask him about.

Especially now in the spring when there was so much to attend to and change everywhere.

But there *was* something wrong. Maybe he wasn't content with the farm at Kiær's; it was said that he was difficult to work with.

But she had dark moods once in a while too.

That was probably because she wasn't getting enough sleep.

She would stay in the parlor in the evening when Bai got

undressed. He walked around half-naked for such a long time, and sat on the edge of the bed, talking, and never seemed to finish.

It seemed to Katinka that it took him so long to get to bed and be done with it.

And when she herself went to bed and lay there in the dark next to Bai, who was sleeping soundly, she couldn't fall asleep and felt so uncomfortable that she would get up again and go into the parlor. There she would sit by the window. The night train rushed past, and the vast silence lay once again over the fields. Not a sound, not a breath of wind in the summer night. The first gray dawning of day appeared, and cold, damp air rose from the meadows.

And it would grow lighter and lighter as the larks began to sing.

Huus was so fond of watching the dawn, he said.

He had told her how it was in the mountains when the dawn came. It was like a mighty golden-red sea, he said, part gold and part roses—around all the mountaintops. And the peaks would sail like islands in the great sea.

And then, little by little, he said, all the mountaintops would catch fire.

And then came the sun.

And it rose.

And swept the darkness out of the valleys as if with a great wing.

He often talked about things like that now, about things from his travels.

He generally talked more now—when he talked at all.

It grew quite light, and Katinka was still sitting at the window. But she ought to go to bed.

The air was heavy in the bedroom, and Bai had thrown off all the covers.

When Huus came over in the evening, they would usually sit in the gazebo beneath the elder.

They watched the eight o'clock train leave. A single farmer had sauntered out onto the platform and greeted them as he walked past and went homeward.

Then they went down to the garden. The cherry trees were in bloom. The white petals drifted down like a light, glittering rain through the summer air onto the lawn.

They sat quietly and looked out at the white trees. The evening's soft silence across the plateau seemed to wrap itself around everything. Up in the village a door slammed. The cattle lowed across the fields.

Katinka talked about her home.

About her girlfriends and her brothers and the old courtyard that was full of doves.

"And later—in the new apartment—with Mother—after Father died . . . Yes, that was a happy time.

"But then I got married, you know."

Huus gazed out over the soft snow of the fruit blossoms that were falling so gently onto the grass.

"Thora Berg, how merry she was . . . In the evening, when she was coming home from a party—with the whole garrison at her heels—she would throw sand at all the windows in town."

Katinka sat for a moment.

"She's married now too," she said. "With a lot of children, they say."

A man walked past on the road outside. "Good evening," he said over the hedge.

"Good evening, Kristen Peder."

"Good evening," said Katinka.

"Hm . . ." said Katinka again, "the last time I saw her was at my wedding. The young girls sang, they stood next to the organ, up by the pulpit. I can still see them now—all their faces—all of them . . . But how I cried . . ."

Huus still said nothing, and she couldn't see his face. He was sitting bent over and studying something on the ground.

"It's almost eleven years ago," said Katinka. "Yes, time flies . . ."

"When you're happy," said Huus without moving.

Katinka didn't hear him at first. Then it was as if his words suddenly caught up with her.

"Yes," she said, shivering a little.

And a little later:

"This is where my home is, after all."

They sat in silence once again.

Bai came into the garden. You could hear him from far away. He always made so much noise—and it had been so quiet before, in the twilight.

"I'll go get the glasses," said Katinka.

"Yes, a lovely evening," said Bai, "a lovely evening out in the open."

Katinka came back with glasses and a bottle.

"I've had a visitor," said Bai.

"Who was it?"

"Miss Ida. She's going away now."

"What—Ida?"

"Yes"—and Bai laughed—"they've given up on Miss Louise. Now they're setting all their sails on the lighter ship. She'll be gone the whole summer. Oh well—if only it would work out for one of them." Bai sat there for a bit. "Well, what the hell—a girl like that has to get married . . ."

Bai often expounded on weddings and marriage. He was something of a philosopher on that subject.

"*I* took a position with the railroad," he said. "Do you think it was because I wanted to? But it didn't work out as a lieutenant. That's the way it is, there are no excuses. Girls have to go to the bridal altar . . . And that's how it goes—you can see it—they get used to each other. They have a house and a home and then come the children . . .

"For most of them," concluded Bai with a small sigh.

They sat in silence; it had grown quite dark beneath the elder.

It was the end of June.

"The lovely woman is looking so peaked," said Agnes Linde when she came down to the station.

"Yes—I suppose I can't tolerate the heat," said Katinka. It was as if she had a restlessness in her blood, and she was always starting things and giving them up again and bustling around.

Most of all she liked to sit with Agnes by the river. She would gaze out over the meadows and always listen to the same thing.

Agnes Linde had a completely different, gentle voice when she talked about him.

"That man," as she called him.

Katinka would sit looking at her as Agnes sat there with bowed head, smiling.

"And then you complain," said Agnes. "That monster . . . because things are the way they are—and perhaps *that* is the best you will have . . ."

"Yes," said Katinka and continued looking at her.

Whenever Agnes Linde didn't come to visit her, Katinka would go up to the parsonage. She actually longed to hear her speak.

And then she would see Andersen too. She saw them together, Agnes and him.

She stood nearby while they played croquet on the big lawn. She stood and watched them—those two who *loved each other*.

She watched and listened to them with curiosity—they were almost like a great mystery.

And one day she wept as she walked home.

Huus came over so irregularly now. Sometimes he would come twice a day and had barely sat down in the gazebo before he would have to take to his horse again. And then half a week at a time would pass when they wouldn't see him at the station at all.

It was the hay harvest, he said.

The hay had been cut and now stood in stacks across the meadows. There was a spicy fragrance in the air everywhere.

One evening Huus was in a good mood and suggested that they should "go on a picnic to the big fair." Drive over in the wagon and rest in the woods first, and then see all the wonders at the fair.

Bai was amenable. And the trip was agreed upon. They would leave early in the morning while it was still cool and not return home until late at night or the next morning.

Just the Bais and Huus.

Katinka was busy all day with preparations.

She studied her cookbook and thought about it at night, and then went to town herself to buy the food.

Huus arrived for the mail just as the train was pulling away.

"Huus!" she called from her compartment.

"But where are you going?" he shouted.

"Shopping. Marie is going too." And she pulled Marie over and showed her face in the window. "Goodbye."

"Hm," said Bai, "Katinka has gone a little crazy. She's cooking and frying for that picnic as if she wanted to keep us from getting cholera."

In town they had started putting up the tents in the streets; in the market square stood the carousel horses, leaning in rows against the wall of the church. Katinka walked around among the market vendors, who were hammering and pounding, and looked at everything. She stared at the crates and stood daydreaming in front of every piece of sailcloth that was hauled up.

"If the young miss wouldn't mind moving . . ."

She had to jump over planks and ropes.

"They called me 'miss,' " she said. "Marie, if only the weather will hold."

They walked down the streets to the park. A gypsy wagon was parked there. The men were sleeping in the ditch, and a woman was washing stockings in a basin on the fold-down steps. Three pair of white unmentionables hung full-length and flapping from a line.

Katinka peered inquisitively at the woman and at the men in the ditch.

"Something you want?" shouted the woman in broken Danish.

"Oh!" cried Katinka; she was quite frightened and ran off.

"That was the Strong Woman," she said.

They walked farther along the road. At the edge of the woods a group of carpenters was building a dance floor. It was cool there under the trees after the sunny road. Katinka sat down on a bench.

"Here's where we're going to dance," she said.

"Yes, he must be a wonderful dancer, that Huus," said Marie. She was still a steadfast admirer of Huus; his picture stood in a velvet frame on her dresser, and an old visiting card with his name on it was the bookmark in her hymnal. Railroad Peter took care of her more down-to-earth needs.

Katinka didn't reply. She just sat there gazing at the men working.

"If only this weather holds," she said to one of them.

"Yes," he said, looking up into the trees—he couldn't see the sky—as he wiped off the sweat with his sleeve, "that's what counts."

Katinka and Marie walked back. It was getting late. They

crossed the market square; the evening bells were ringing from the tower, cutting through the noise of the marketplace.

On the last day they baked. Katinka had her sleeves pushed up and was kneading so that she had flour in her hair like a miller.

"Don't let anyone in—don't let anyone in." Someone was knocking on the door, which was locked.

Katinka thought it was Huus.

"It's me," shouted Agnes Linde. "What's going on?"

She came in and helped them bake. There was a pound cake that had to be stirred forever. "It's for Huus," said Katinka. "He's going to have pound cake for his sweet tooth."

Agnes Linde stirred so the dough bubbled. "Yes, those men *have* to have their pound cake," she said.

Katinka took out the cookie sheet. "Taste one," she said. "They're piping hot." She was as flushed as a copper pot from the oven.

Miss Jensen and Big Louise came down for the afternoon train. There was stamping and chattering in front of the kitchen window.

"God help me, they must have smelled it," said Agnes Linde. She let her arms drop wearily and sat down quite ungracefully with the bowl of dough between her widespread legs.

Marie took a plate with some samples on it out to them on the platform.

Louise kicked her legs with glee from the platform bench so that a couple of mercantile agents in the train saw a significant portion of her "beauty."

When the train had gone, the women in the kitchen opened the windows. Big Louise and Little Jensen were munching away out on the bench.

"You're so lucky, Mrs. Bai, incredible . . ."

"Yes, Mrs. Bai is the mistress of *her* house," said Miss Jensen.

"There goes the chatterbox," said Agnes in the kitchen. She started in on the dough again.

Bai opened the office window above the platform bench.

"So," he said, "here *I* sit with an empty stomach."

"Would you like some, Mr. Bai?" asked Louise. "Are you fond of sweets too?"

"If anyone would spare me some," said Bai in his club tone of voice.

There was a commotion and little shrieks from the platform.

"What's going on?" yelled Agnes from the kitchen.

"We're feeding the bird," said Big Louise. She had jumped up on the bench with her "beauty" and was standing there putting cookies into Bai's mouth.

"Ooh, he bites," she yelled.

On such occasions Mrs. Abel would say: "They never grow up; when you don't know anything about the world . . ."

Big Louise brought back the empty plate. She snapped up the crumbs with the tips of her fingers. The Misses Abel were always like that: they never left anything.

She stood at the kitchen window and looked inside.

"Mother should have known about this," she said sweetly.

"So she didn't sniff it out," said Agnes over the pound cake.

Big Louise was handed a paper cone full of cookies through the window. "There's enough to save some too," she said when she got out onto the road with Little Jensen.

She and Miss Jensen devoured the cookies before they passed the woods. Big Louise threw away the paper.

"God, little Louise . . . Miss Linde with those eyes . . . she might see you . . ."

Miss Jensen picked up the paper. In her pocket she quietly twisted it around three cookies for Bel-Ami.

Katinka was starting to feel tired. She sat down on the butcher block with her rolled-up sleeves and regarded her work.

"But this is nothing compared to home—nothing compared to when we baked for Christmas."

She talked about how they had baked—her mother and her sisters and the whole house. She made pigs out of *klejner* dough. Wham—and then they would split when they were dropped into the hot oil.

And her brothers—they went around stealing so that her mother had to use her big wooden spoon to guard the stone crock full of ginger-snap dough.

And if they peeled almonds, they would steal so many that less than fifty would be left from a whole pound.

Someone was knocking on the door. It was Huus.

"No one can come in," said Katinka at the door. "In an hour . . . Come back in an hour."

Huus appeared at the window. "You can wait in the garden," said Katinka. She rushed to finish up and sent Agnes out to keep Huus company.

Agnes stayed for half an hour. Then she left.

"It's too easy to keep Foreman Huus company," she told Andersen. "He only asks that you keep quiet so he can whistle in peace."

"Where's Agnes?" asked Katinka when she came down to the garden.

"She left, I think."

"But when?"

"It must be about an hour ago." Huus started to laugh. "Miss Linde and I are very fond of each other. But we don't have that much to *say* to each other."

"We have to pack," said Katinka.

They went inside and started packing the large basket. They padded everything with hay so the crocks wouldn't tip over.

"Tighter," said Katinka, "tighter." And she pressed her hands against his.

She opened her desk and counted out the spoons and forks from the silver chest.

"And I'm going to take a fan along," she said.

She began to search for it. "Oh, it's in the drawer."

It was the drawer with the cotillion boxes and the bridal veil. She opened the box with the old bits of ribbon. "Look," she said, "all this old junk."

She put her hand into the box and rummaged through the ribbons and medallions like a millwheel. "This old junk."

She was still looking for the fan.

"Oh, hold my veil," she said. She put the bridal veil and a shawl over Huus's arm. "*There* it is." The fan was at the bottom of the drawer.

"And your shawl," she said. It lay to one side, wrapped in tissue paper. She took it out.

Huus had clutched the yellowish bridal veil so tightly that he left marks in the bobbinet.

The evening train arrived, and they went out on the platform.

"Whew," said the slim train conductor in the tight pants, "getting a train through during the holidays . . . half an hour late . . ."

"It's a sweaty business," said Bai.

Katinka looked down the length of the train. A perspiring face was sticking out of every window.

"Yes," she said. "To think these people want to travel." The conductor started laughing.

"Well," he said, "that's what railroads are for." He gave the two-finger signal and sprang up onto the step.

The train pulled away. The young conductor kept on standing there leaning forward, laughing and nodding.

Katinka waved with her blue shawl. And from the compartment windows all the people on holiday were suddenly waving and nodding; they laughed and joked and called hello.

Katinka shouted and swung the entire shawl; and from the train they replied for as long as they could see her.

After tea, Huus drove home. He would be at the station tomorrow at six o'clock.

Katinka stood in the garden in front of the hedge.

> Cricket, cricket, fly away, fly away.
> Cricket, cricket,
> Bring good weather today . . .

she called.

The scent from the trees in the grove drifted down toward her. She stood there smiling and gazing up into the blue sky.

Blue sure suits that little woman, thought the train conductor with the tight pants. He was always on the lookout for what he might find along the train line.

"We have to get up at five o'clock," said Bai out in the kitchen.

"Yes, yes, Bai, I'm coming now." Katinka scraped a burnt spot off the pound cake. "I just have to finish . . ."

She wrapped up the pound cake and checked the basket one last time. She opened the door to the courtyard and stood looking out. The doves were cooing up there. That was the only sound.

In the sky toward the west the last pale pink was vanishing. The river was twisting its way through the steaming meadows.

How she loved this place . . .

She closed the door and went inside.

Bai had set his watch beside the burning candle next to the bed. He had wanted to keep an eye on how long her "dawdling" would take.

But he had fallen asleep and lay there sweating and snoring in the glow of the candle.

Katinka quietly put it out. She undressed in the dark.

Katinka was in the garden when the wagon arrived. Her
blue dress was visible all the way to the bend in the road.

"Good morning, good morning... You bring good
weather."

She ran out onto the platform. "He's here," she called.
"The baskets, Marie."

Bai was in his shirtsleeves in the bedroom window.
"Morning, Huus, looks like a scorcher, doesn't it?"

"Oh, there's a slight breeze," said Huus, getting out of the
wagon.

They got the baskets lashed on and drank coffee out on the
platform. Little Bentzen was so sleepy that Bai made him run
"ready to attack" up and down the platform three times to
wake him up.

Katinka promised to bring a gingerbread heart home for
him, and they got into the wagon. Bai wanted to drive the
horses and sat on the front seat with Marie, whose clothes
were so starched that they crackled whenever she moved.

Katinka looked like a young girl in her big white sun hat.

"They're bringing over food for you from the inn," said
Katinka to Little Bentzen.

"Now we're off," said Bai. Little Bentzen ran into the
garden and waved and waved.

They drove along a side road for a while through the
fields. It was still cool, with a cheerful summer breeze; the
clover and the damp grass were so fragrant.

"How fresh it is," said Katinka.

"Yes, a lovely morning," said Huus.

"Nice breeze blowing." Bai flicked at the horses.

They rolled out onto the main road past Kiær's property.
The wagon where the herdsman lived stood on its wheels in
the midst of the cattle. In the distance a dog was chasing after
some cattle; the big cows lifted their thick necks and lowed,
sluggish and contented.

Katinka gazed out across the green field with the scattered cattle glistening in the sunshine.

"How beautiful it is," she said.

"Yes, isn't it?" said Huus, turning toward her. "It *is* beautiful."

They began to talk—Katinka and Huus. They noticed and enjoyed the same things. Their eyes always fell on exactly the same things. And then either he or Katinka would nod.

Bai was talking to the beasts like an old cavalryman.

An hour hadn't passed before he began to talk about "having a snack."

"The morning makes a man hungry, Tik," he said. "Have to have something to keep you going."

Katinka really couldn't unpack everything now, and where would they sit?

But Bai wouldn't let up, and they stopped next to a field where the rye was gathered in bundles.

They took one of the baskets out of the wagon and sat down on a bundle close to the ditch.

Bai ate as if he hadn't seen food for a week.

"*Skaal*, Huus," he said. "Here's to good company."

They talked and passed around the crocks and ate.

"That's more like it, Tik," said Bai.

People went by on the road and stared at them.

"Sure looks good," they said and walked on.

"*Skaal*, Huus, here's to you."

"Thank you, Mrs. Bai."

"That helped a lot," said Bai. They were in the wagon again. "But it sure is hot, isn't it, Marie?"

"Yes," said Marie, her face glistening, "it's hot."

"We'll be getting to the woods soon," said Huus.

They drove on. Ahead lay the edge of the woods, swathed in blue from the heat.

"Smell how fragrant the fir trees are," said Katinka.

They reached the fringe of the woods, and the dense firs cast a shadow far across the road. They all took a deep breath, but they didn't speak as they drove slowly through the woods. From the road the firs stood in long straight rows that ended in darkness. And no birds, no songs, no sound.

Only insects, which hovered in great clouds up in the light, away from the trees.

They came out of the woods again.

"Pretty solemn in there, wasn't it?" Bai broke the silence.

Around noon they reached the beech woods and went into the forester's house.

Bai said, "It feels good to stretch. A man has to stretch his legs, Huus." And he went over and sat down to sleep under a tree.

Huus helped with the unpacking. "You have such nimble fingers, Huus," said Katinka. Marie went back and forth and warmed up the crocks in hot water in the kitchen.

"That's what my mother-in-law always said," said Huus.

"Your mother-in-law..."

"Yes," said Huus, "my fiancée's mother..."

Katinka said nothing. Knives and forks clattered out of the paper she was holding.

"Yes," said Huus, "I've never told you about that. I was engaged once."

"Really? I didn't know that."

Katinka set the knives in place. Marie came back.

"We could walk down to the pond," said Huus.

"All right, if Marie will call us." They walked along the path into the woods. The pond was a marshy lake a short way in; the trees stretched their great crowns out over the dark water.

They hadn't spoken along the way. Now they were sitting next to each other on a bench in front of the lake.

"No," said Huus, "I've never talked about it."

Katinka stared silently out over the water.

"My mother was the one," he said, "who wanted it so badly . . . for the sake of my future."

"I see," said Katinka.

"So it was . . . a whole year . . . before she called it off."

Huus spoke hesitantly, with long pauses, as if ashamed or angry.

"That's the way it is," he continued, "with engagements and marriages."

A bird began to warble within the woods. Katinka heard every single note in the silence.

"And then, on top of it all, a man's a coward and stays involved in it," Huus went on. "Such a profoundly lazy coward . . . day after day.

"I stayed in it"—his voice was low—"until *she* called it off . . . Because she was fond of me."

Katinka placed her hand, softly caressing, on his, which he was pressing hard against the bench.

"Poor Huus," was all she said.

And she sat there patting his hand, gently and soothingly: the poor man, how he had suffered.

They sat like that, close to each other. The noon heat hovered over the water of the little lake. Mosquitoes and flies buzzed in swarms.

They spoke no more. Marie's call awakened them.

"They're calling," said Katinka.

They stood up and silently walked up the path.

They were all so merry at lunch. Afterwards they drank the old Aalborg port with the pound cake.

Bai sat in his shirtsleeves and every other minute he said: "Well, children, it's damned nice in the green Danish woods."

He was seized with a fit of tenderness and wanted Katinka to sit on his lap. She tore herself away. "Bai, please!" she said. She turned pale and blushed at the same time.

"I suppose you're shy in front of strangers," said Bai.

Silence had fallen. Katinka began to pack up the baskets and Huus stood up.

"Yes," said Bai, "how about a walk after lunch." He put on his coat. "Ought to help the digestion."

"Yes," said Katinka, "you two could take a little walk while I pack up."

Huus and Bai went along the road. Bai walked with his hat in his hand. He was warm from the heat and the old port wine.

"You see that, Huus? That's marriage for you, by God," he said. "That's the way it is, and no different.

"It does no damned good—what everyone keeps writing, and what you sit and swill down in that reading club about marriage and chastity and all that... and fidelity and—'needs'! They're just as stuffy about those as old Linde is when he says the Lord's Prayer.

"It's all nicely put and it sounds good—and it gives those folks something to write about. But the thing is, it doesn't get to the crux of the matter, don't you see, Huus..."

He stopped and made a sweeping gesture with his straw hat in front of Huus.

"You saw it for yourself: I have desires—and Katinka doesn't want to... lovely summer day, we've had a good meal out in the woods, but it makes no difference... not even a kiss.

"That's the way women are... You can't ever count on them. They only feel like it occasionally, you see, Huus...

"Just between us," Bai shook his head, "it can be damned difficult for a man in the prime of his life."

Huus struck some nettles aside with his walking stick. He was swinging it so hard that they snapped, as if they were mowed down.

"Yes, that's the problem," said Bai, who walked along looking thoughtful the whole time. "But they sure don't talk about that in the reading club. But between us men—*we* know where the shoe pinches."

They heard Katinka calling behind them, and Huus answered with a shout that resounded through the woods.

Katinka was feeling cheerful again: shouldn't they take a little nap under the trees? She knew a place, a lovely spot beneath an old oak tree. And she led the way to find it.

Huus followed her. He made a noise like a cuckoo through the trees. Bai heard him laughing and yodeling.

"Well, he can go ahead and laugh—he's outside of it all."

A little later Bai was asleep under the big oak with his nose in the air and his hat lying on his stomach.

"You should sleep now, Huus," said Katinka.

"All right . . ." said Huus. They were sitting on either side of the tree trunk.

Katinka had taken off her straw hat and was leaning her head against the oak. She sat there gazing up into the tree. In the very top of its crown the sunbeams fell like dripping drops of gold into the green . . . And the birds were singing in the underbrush.

"How beautiful it is here," she whispered, bending her head forward.

"Yes—it's beautiful here . . ." repeated Huus in a whisper. He was sitting with his arms around his knees and staring up into the crown of the tree.

It was so quiet. They both heard Bai breathing; a buzzing insect that they followed with their eyes up toward the green branches; and the birds that were chirping, first close at hand, then farther off.

"Are you asleep?" whispered Katinka.

"Yes," said Huus.

They didn't move. Huus listened, then stood up cautiously and took a step forward. Yes, she was sleeping. She looked like a child with her head tilted and her mouth slightly open, smiling in her sleep.

Huus stood there for a long time looking at her. Then he quietly returned to his place and, with his eyes gazing up at the oak, he happily listened to her sleeping.

When Marie woke them up for coffee with several mighty shouts, Bai had slept off his annoyance along with the old port.

"A cognac goes good in the woods," he said. "A nice little cognac in the woods."

With that little cognac Bai had another piece of pound cake. Bai was a man with a big appetite.

"Wonderful cake," he said.

"It's Huus's cake," said Katinka.

"Well, yes," said Bai, "just as long as the rest of us can have a bite . . ."

After coffee they drove off. Bai was tired of holding the reins, and he took Huus's place on the back seat with Katinka. They were all feeling a little drowsy—the hot summer sun beat down, and there was dust on the road too. Katinka sat and stared at Huus's neck, broad and quite tan from the sun.

The courtyard of the hotel was crowded with empty, un-hitched wagons. Women and girls who had just climbed down from the wagon seats were shaking out their skirts and smoothing them down. All of the windows of the cellar room were open; the steaming punch was flowing amply at the card game. A falsetto with piano was busy with "My Valdemar" in the parlor wing behind the rolled-down shades.

"That's one of Agnes's pieces," said Katinka.

"That's the Nightingales," said Bai. "Tonight we'll have to go in and hear them warble."

Katinka kept close to the parlor wing as they walked. But there was nothing to see.

"No peeking," said Bai. "Admission at the ticket window."

Behind the curtains a woman's voice began with a shriek to invoke "My Charles":

> Oh, my Charles—
> send me a letter please—

"Oh," said Katinka; she stood there at the window and nodded. "That's the one. Agnes knows that one."

> And set my heart at ease . . .

"Come on, Tik," said Bai. "Walk with Huus. I'll clear the way when it gets too crowded."

"But we can never remember more than the first verse," said Katinka. She kept listening as she took Huus's arm.

> And set my heart at ease . . .

implored the shrieking teakettle.

"It's usually just more of the same thing in the other ones," said Huus.

"Are you coming?" shouted Bai.

Outside the gate a staggering old woman was singing about Thomas the mass murderer and beating his effigy with a cane. The spectators were standing there looking sheepish and repeating the refrain, dragging it out like an amen in church.

The girls were walking arm in arm in long rows with rigid expressions past the young men, who were looking them over, standing in huddles in front of the tents, smoking pipes, with their hands stuffed in their pockets.

One young man stepped forward.

"Hello, Mary," he said.

And Mary gave him the tips of her fingers: "Hello, Søren," she said. And the whole row of girls stopped and waited.

Søren stood for a moment in front of Mary, looking first at his pipe and then at his boots. "Goodbye, Mary," he said.

"Goodbye, Søren."

And Søren went back to his group, and the row of girls closed ranks again, walking on with pursed lips.

"Hell of a way to block the street," said Bai.

The women gathered in groups and stood there with sad faces, as if they were at a funeral, sizing up each other. When they spoke, they whispered inaudibly, as though they couldn't really open their mouths, and after they had uttered a couple of words they would fall silent again, standing there looking quietly offended.

It was impossible to make any headway. "I'm using my elbows," said Katinka. She was constantly being shoved into Huus.

"Just keep close to me," said Huus.

It was impossible to hear anything because of the staggering mass murderess and a couple of barrel organs that were sadly blending General Bertrand's farewell song with the duet of the Ajaxes. Schoolboys were dashing in and out of the crowd, whistling through their fingers, and lethargic country youths were blowing up balloons and making them screech while they stared into space with blank expressions.

The sun was shining straight down on the street and baking both the people and the gingerbread cakes.

"Whew, it's hot," said Katinka.

"Let's get a cone over here," shouted Bai.

"Cones, madam, cones—made by Tyrolean Ferdinand's brown-eyed daughter."

"Cones, Huus, cones," said Katinka. She pushed her way through a wall of girls who were blocking the street.

The girls squealed. Oh, the schoolboys had pinned their skirts together.

"It's the boys from the Latin school," yelled a couple of louts from the public school. "They used pins to fasten them together."

The girls ran around in a group trying to get loose. "Ooh," they howled, "ooh!" The schoolboys saw their chance and broke in like lightning to pinch the girls on the legs.

"Eek!" There was a great shrieking. Katinka screamed along too, out of giddiness.

"Cones, madam, cones—made by Tyrolean Ferdinand's brown-eyed daughter."

They stepped up to the oven. "Three cones, sir, Dutch ones, 15 øre."

"Sprinkle on the sugar, you brown-eyed girl."

The brown-eyed girl sprinkled the sugar with her bare fingers. "Yes, madam," said the man, "she's seen better days... How about a tip," and he screamed it out over the street, "for Tyrolean Ferdinand's brown-eyed daughter!"

The brown-eyed girl automatically held out a piggy bank, rattling it and looking as if she neither heard nor saw a thing.

"Sugar, you brown-eyed girl."

The brown-eyed girl's fingers once more grabbed for the sugar.

They reached the fair itself. "I'm going deaf," said Katinka, holding her hands to her ears. Le Tort, the great magic professor, was up on a tall scaffold with two kettledrums struggling against the music from three carousels. A white-painted Pierrot was dragging up a giant drum in front of the world's biggest arena:

"The biggest arena, ladies and gentlemen, the world-famous arena..."

He made music by sitting down hard on his drum with the most posterior part of his body.

"Miss Flora—Miss Flora on the high trapeze..."

It was right in front of them: "Miss Flora—queen of the air—gentlemen—only 10 øre..." The barker was swinging an alarm bell in his right hand.

"Queen of the air—10 øre..."

Professor Le Tort was bitter. He was shouting about all the wonders of the world so that his voice cracked, and he decided to produce the five hundred yards of silk ribbon free of charge. Up on his scaffold he began to regurgitate and pull

tissue-paper streamers out of his throat, turning red in the face
as if he were about to have a stroke.

"Queen of the air—only 10 øre . . ."

In the world's biggest arena Pierrot was standing on his
head on the drum and pounding the drumhead with his skull.

The carousels were turning to the sound of horns and
barrel organs.

"Ladies, queen of the air . . . the queen of the air—10
øre."

There was baking sunshine, the smell of gingerbread
cakes, and the clamor of a shoving throng.

"Oh, it's so lovely," said Katinka. She looked up at Huus
and shivered just a little, like a kitten, in the heat.

"There's that woman," she said.

"Who is she?" asked Huus.

"The one who was washing clothes."

It was the queen of the air who was making her entrance
up the stairs with pink legs in laced boots and a wide, wrig-
gling derrière.

"Miss Flora—the *so-called* queen of the air—10 øre."

The queen of the air had a fan which she handled like a fig
leaf; she chewed on some plums before she had to go inside
and start flying.

"Shall we go in?" asked Katinka.

"Tik!" shouted Bai. He wanted to see the Snake Lady.
They worked their way through the crowd and passed a
carousel. Marie was riding on a lion, almost in the lap of a
cavalryman.

Katinka wanted to ride too. Bai said he wouldn't pay good
money to have his guts churned up. Katinka found a horse on
the inside, next to Huus. They started to turn, slowly, and
then faster. She nodded to Bai and laughed at all the faces that
were swirling past.

"What a crowd," she said. She could see over everybody's
head.

They went around again. "Grab the ring," said Katinka, bending forward across Huus.

"Look out," he said, holding on to her.

Katinka smiled and leaned back. The faces began to blur in front of her. They were just something black—black and white—that kept on turning.

She kept smiling as she closed her eyes.

The noise of the fair and the music and the voices and the screeching horns all seemed to collapse into one big roar in her ears, while everything was gently rocking.

She opened her eyes a little. "I can't see a thing," she said and closed them again.

The bell rang and they turned more slowly. "One more time," she said. They went again. Huus had leaned inward— she didn't know that she was leaning on his shoulder. "Grab it," she said. They flew past the ring and she laughed into his face.

She sat with half-open eyes and gazed into the swirling circles. It seemed as though all the faces were being pulled along on a string.

Dizzy, she recognized Marie—she had gotten back on— in the wagon with her cavalryman. She was sitting on his knee. The way she looked—almost swooning . . .

And all the others—the way they *leaned*—as if they were half dead—against the young men . . .

Katinka suddenly straightened up: all the blood had rushed to her head. The carousel stopped.

"Come on," she said. She got down from the horse.

Bai was standing next to the pole with the ring; Katinka took his hand. "It makes me dizzy," she said, stepping down onto the ground. She was quite pale from all that riding in circles.

"Huus, help Tik," said Bai. "I'll be your beacon." He pinched Marie on the arm. She was getting down from the carousel with her cavalryman.

Marie was embarrassed to see her master and mistress and gave the blue uniform a swat.

"Splendid—she's a lively one," said Bai as he set out.

"It's right here," said Katinka. Huus offered her his arm.

Miss Theodora, the Snake Lady, was displaying her sluggish animals right next to the carousel. There were several fat, slimy creatures, which she took out of a box of woolen blankets. Miss Theodora tickled them under the chin to make them a little friskier.

"They are digesting, Miss," said Bai in his club tone of voice.

"They're doing *what*?" asked Miss Theodora. "Don't you think these animals are alive?" Miss Theodora took digestion to be an insult.

She tossed the snake around her neck and scratched its head so it opened its jaws and managed to emit a hiss.

Miss Theodora called it her little dear and hugged it to her breast. Miss Theodora had the girth of a giant woman and was wearing a page costume.

The snake quietly let its tail flap between Miss Theodora's knees. "Darling beast," said Miss Theodora.

"Come on," said Katinka, "that's disgusting." She had taken Huus's arm in revulsion.

"Yes," said the owner, who took it as fear and was flattered. "Monstrous beasts, little lady... But she worked with lions once too."

Katinka was outside.

"To think a person could do something like that," she said. She gave a shudder.

"Yes," said Bai, moving his hand around knowledgeably. The owner had challenged "the gentleman" to assure himself that the animals were actually moving about "practically on her naked body."

"Yes," said Bai, "it's flesh all right..."

Reconciled, Miss Theodora the Snake Lady smiled as she put her "darlings" back in the box.

"Yes," said the owner, "she's worked with lions too, sir."

"For eight years, sir," said Miss Theodora.

Huus and Katinka were on the other side of the square. It was gradually getting dark, and all the barkers were howling from their scaffolds, competing with the zeal of desperation.

"Bargain price—bargain price, lady," the professor shouted down at Katinka. He wiped off the sweat with his "mysterious handkerchief": "Only 20 øre with your sweetheart . . ."

Katinka walked faster, so Bai could hardly catch up with them.

People began to grow merrier. Reeling, singing groups of young men ran into the rows of girls, which dissolved with a squeal; and couples were starting to embrace here and there along the tent streets.

There was a great noise coming from the refreshment tents and from up near the brown-eyed girl, where cognac was being served with the cones.

The three police officers were limping by with canes. They had been slightly wounded in the wars and they stuck together to keep order. Around behind the tents and in groups the abrupt whistling of the schoolboys was heard piercing through the noise.

It was growing darker and darker as Katinka and Huus strolled past the tents, buying things.

In the tents they were already lighting the storm lanterns, which shone dimly over the hearts and gingerbread cakes. The women behind the high counters were polishing the gingerbread cakes with the palms of their hands so they shone, and handed them down to Huus and Katinka on a long spatula.

Bai appeared and bought some too.

Huus had bought Katinka a little Japanese tray as a souvenir of the fair. She gave him a gingerbread cake.

"What?" said Bai. "Are you giving Huus gingerbread cakes? . . . Give him a heart! Madam," he shouted, "a heart here!"

"One heart, sir—with a verse . . ."

"Bai," said Katinka.

"Looks like a shower on the way," said Huus behind them.

"The devil you say." Bai turned around from the counter.

The first drops fell. "It's going to be a downpour," said Bai.

"Let's go into the Panorama," said Huus.

"All right." Katinka took Bai's arm. "Come on," she said.

People were running into all the doorways. Women and girls threw their skirts over their heads or ran holding their handkerchiefs over their new hats.

"Hey, hey," said Bai, "here come the petticoats."

The girls were standing around in the doorways, blue-stockinged and with their Icelandic woolen petticoats against the doorposts.

The tradespeople hauled in their wares, swearing and cursing. The schoolboys dashed off screeching, letting themselves get soaked.

"Here it is," said Katinka.

"All of Italy, folks, for 50 øre." The man was hoarse and bundled up in woolen scarves. "Three tickets—go on in."

"Look how it's pouring," said Katinka. She was standing in the tent opening, shaking her clothes and looking out.

The water was sluicing down. There was already flooding across half the marketplace. The slightly injured police were limping hurriedly around beneath umbrellas and lifting gutter planks.

All around under tents and in doorways stood partially wet females, looking disheveled.

Inside the Panorama it was empty and very quiet. The heavy, monotonous beat of the rain could be heard on the roof, and it had grown so cool.

Katinka seemed to be catching her breath after all that noise.

"Oh, that feels good," she said.

"It's different parts of the country," said Bai, who had started to peer into the peepholes.

"The blue water," he said, moving on. He preferred to go out into the entryway to see what might show up under the Icelandic petticoats.

Katinka remained seated. She felt herself newborn in here, alone with Huus in the silence under the falling rain.

"They're not playing," she said.

"No, because of the rain . . ."

They both listened to the rain falling.

"What a commotion there was," she said.

Katinka would have preferred to stay sitting there, quietly listening to the rain. But she stood up anyway. "Is it Italy?" she asked.

"That's what he said."

She looked into a peephole. "Yes," she said, "it's Italy."

There was artificial light inside, in front of the pictures, which shone with bright colors.

"It's so beautiful."

"That's the gulf," said Huus, "near Naples."

The picture wasn't bad. Glittering sunshine lay over the gulf and the beach and the city. Boats flew across the blue of the water.

"Naples," said Katinka more softly.

She continued to peer inside. Huus looked into the next peephole at the same picture.

"Have you been there?"

"Yes—two months."

"Sailing there?" said Katinka.

"Yes—to Sorrento."

"Sorrento . . ." Katinka softly repeated the foreign name, lingeringly. "Oh," she said, "to travel."

They walked along the peepholes and looked in at pictures side by side. The rain fell fainter against the roof—finally only intermittent drops.

They looked at Rome, the Forum, and the Colosseum. Huus told her about them.

"It's so magnificent," said Katinka, "that it's frightening."

"I like Naples the best . . ."

Outside the barrel organs began to play; the carousels were ringing. Katinka had almost forgotten where she was.

"It's probably not raining anymore."

"No, it's stopped."

Katinka looked around the room. "Bai must be waiting," she said.

She walked back and looked one more time at the bay near Naples with the racing boats.

Bai came in and said that the street was once again filled with crowds.

"Time for the woods, don't you think?" he asked.

They left. The air was clean and cool. Large, happy groups of people were moving along the road toward the woods.

The trees and the hawthorn thickets smelled fragrant after the rain.

The sun went down, and the colored lanterns were lit on the arch over the entrance to the woods. The young men were heading that way with their arms around the girls' waists. All the benches along the road were full. In tender poses they sat and courted in secret.

They began to hear the music from the dance floor and the humming sound of many voices.

"Now we'll have us a dance," said Bai.

Outside the dance floor there was a crowd of half-grown fellows and girls who were watching over the railing. On the floor they were stomping a polka so hard it thundered.

"Come on, Tik," said Bai, "let's join the dance."

Bai danced vigorously and kept at it, in and out among the other couples.

"Bai, please!" said Katinka. She was out of breath.

"I can still swing it, all right," said Bai. He was dancing the wrong way and pumping his arm up and down.

"Bai, please . . ."

"I can still make her warm," said Bai. They went over to Huus.

"Have to keep in practice," he said, clicking his heels the way he had at the club dances, "and handle the ladies."

Bai made Katinka feel so uncomfortable.

"Bai is so frisky," she said when he had gone.

"Would you dance once with me?" asked Huus.

"Yes—in a moment—let's wait a while . . ."

They watched Bai pumping away with a buxom peasant girl wearing a velvet shirtwaist.

"Let's take a walk," said Katinka.

They walked away from the dance floor, a little way down the road where the music faded out.

Katinka sat down. "Sit down," she said. "A body gets so tired."

It was so quiet in the woods. Only a few scattered notes reached them now and then. They sat in silence. Huus was drawing on the ground with a stick.

"Where is she now?" asked Katinka suddenly. She was sitting there looking down.

"She?"

"Yes—your fiancée . . ."

"She's married—thank God."

"Thank God?"

"Yes—a man always feels responsible—when a woman sits there . . ."

"But it wasn't your fault . . ." Katinka was silent for a moment. "If she was fond of you."

"She was fond of me," said Huus. "I know that now."

Katinka stood up. "Does she have any children?" she asked when they were farther down the road.

"Yes, a little boy."

They didn't speak again until they reached the dance floor. "Shall we dance?" asked Katinka.

The small lanterns were lit all around, casting only a dim

light over the benches along the side. The couples were swinging out into the light and back again into darkness; on the dance floor it was all a restless blackness, gliding in and out.

Huus and Katinka began to dance. Huus danced calmly, leading with confidence. Katinka felt as though she were resting there in his arms.

She heard everything—the music and the voices and the stamping—as if it were quite far away, and she was only aware of him leading her so securely, in and out.

Huus kept on dancing in that same quiet manner. Katinka noticed that her heart was pounding and that her cheeks were burning. But she didn't ask him to stop and she didn't say a word.

They continued to dance.

"Can you see the sky?" asked Katinka suddenly.

"No," said Huus, "the trees are hiding it."

"So the trees are hiding it," whispered Katinka.

They danced.

"Huus," she said. She looked up at him and didn't know why her eyes filled with tears. "I'm tired."

Huus stopped and put his arm around her to guide her through the crowd.

"We're having fun," said Bai. He twirled past them by the entrance.

They stepped down from the floor and walked along a path.

It was quite dark among the trees; it seemed to be hotter again after the rain, and a penetrating scent from the blossoming hawthorns wafted toward them.

Among the trees and in the underbrush there was a whispering and a rustling, and embracing couples hid on the benches in the darkness.

"Huus, Bai is probably waiting for us," said Katinka. "Come on."

They turned around.

"Well," said Bai, "time to go hear the screaming teaket-
tles. There are some 'songstresses' over in the pavilion—nice
girls, they say... I just have to polka farewell with that little
country girl over there first. Take Katinka for a swing, Huus.
So she doesn't just sit."

Huus put his arm around Katinka and they danced again.

Katinka didn't know whether they had been dancing for a
minute or an hour when they walked through the woods toward the pavilion.

Five women were singing at them from the door. They
kicked up their tassled boots and held two fingers over their
hearts:

> Here come we
> the happy company
> against man's tyranny...

"Here's a cozy corner," said Bai. "We can see the ladies
from here."

They sat down. The faces around them were hardly visible
because of the smoke and vapors. The five women sang about
bayonets and bravery. When they had finished, they drank
punch and flirted by sticking rose petals in their bodices and
giggling behind some crumpled fans.

"Nice girls," said Bai.

Katinka hardly heard him; Huus was sitting with his head
in his hands, staring at the dirty floor.

A little pianist who looked like a grasshopper leaped up to
the piano as if he wanted to play it with his thin nose.

The women were quarreling over "who was going to..."

"It's your turn, Julie," they whispered angrily behind the
fans. "God knows—it's Julie's turn."

"The Chimneysweep," said Julie loudly over the crowd.

"That's *forbidden*," screamed a couple of the women
behind their fans near the pianist. "Sørensen, she's singing a
forbidden song."

Down in the hall they were clinking glasses.

"Ha, just because Josephine can't sing it."

Julie sang "The Chimneysweep":

> August the chimneysweep—
> has a broom for a shield . . .

Bai pounded the table so hard he was just about to break the toddy glasses.

"How about that, Tik," he said.

Katinka gave a start; she hadn't been listening at all. "Oh yes," she said.

"Great," said Bai, "great!" He clapped again.

"Romantic songstress Miss Mathilde Nielsen," shouted Miss Julie.

The romantic singer Miss Mathilde Nielsen was solemn and dressed in a long skirt. The other women said: "Mathilde has a voice." Mathilde had fallen as a child and had broken her nose.

During the prelude she immediately placed her hand over her heart.

"This is the song about Sorrento."

> Where the tall and murky pine
> Lends its shadow to the peasant's vine,
> Where by the gulf the orange grove
> Smells so lovely in the evening mauve;
> Where by the strand the boat does rock,
> Where in the town the happy flock
> Dances while a song they raise,
> Singing loud the Madonna's praise.
> Never, never, shall I forget
> These hills and dales where once we met,
> These limpid moonlit nights,
> Napoli—your paradise.

Miss Mathilde Nielsen sang sentimentally with long, tremulous notes.

When the song was over, the "ladies" applauded by striking their fans against the palms of their hands.

The romantic singer "Miss" Nielsen thanked the audience with a bow.

"Damned if Tik isn't blubbering over the 'ballad,' " said Bai. Katinka was actually sitting there with tears in her eyes.

They went outside. "Now we'll walk back through the cemetery," said Bai.

"Through the cemetery?" said Katinka.

"Yes—it's the easiest way—and it's so beautiful."

Katinka and Huus walked together, following after Bai. They came out of the woods and walked down a tree-lined avenue. The noise and music faded away behind them.

"Yes," said Bai, "a lively day—a day well spent." He kept on chattering: about the dance ("they sure have fun, those country kids") and the "ladies," and "Miss Julie" ("that lively girl in the boots, that saucy girl") and about Marie: "Well— we'll see what that was all about . . . I know her . . ."

The other two didn't say a word. Neither of them paid any attention to him either. It was so quiet that they could hear their own footsteps on the ground. At the end of the road loomed the iron gate of the cemetery with its big cross.

"But Bai," said Katinka.

"Do you think there are ghosts here?" asked Bai. He opened the side gate.

They went in. Katinka took Huus's arm at the entrance. The cemetery lay in the dawn light like a big garden. Roses and boxwood hedges and jasmine and lindens gave off a heavy scent, and gray and white stones rose up between the low hedges.

Katinka held on tightly to Huus's arm as they walked.

Bai went on ahead. He trudged along the shrubbery, flapping his arms as if he were chasing chickens.

Katinka stopped: "Oh, look."

The trees had been cut so that you could look out across the fields to the fjord. The dawn light hovered like a veil over the dark, shiny mirror of the water, calm and dreaming.

It was quiet, as if life had died out beneath that scent-laden air . . . Motionless, they stood there close together.

Slowly they walked on. Katinka would stop now and then to read the inscriptions on the stones shining in the dawn light. She read them—names and years—in a soft, quivering voice.

"Beloved and missed."

"Beloved beyond the grave."

"Love is the fulfilling of the law."

She stepped closer and lifted the branches of the weeping willow; she wanted to read the name on the stone.

Then there was a rustling behind the willow.

"Huus," she said, clutching at his arm.

Something took flight over the fence.

"It was two people," said Huus.

"Oh, I was so scared," said Katinka. She held her hands to her breast.

She kept huddling close to him as her heart pounded.

They didn't say another word. Now there was a rustling in the shrubbery, and Katinka gave a start.

"My little friend, my little friend," whispered Huus as if to a child. Katinka's hand trembled under his.

Bai was standing at the end of the path.

"Are you there?" he asked.

He opened the gate. It clanked into the iron latch behind them.

Out on the road Bai took Huus aside.

"It was just scandalous," he said. "To think that something like that could happen—a desecration of a holy place . . . Kiær told me about this . . . the way things were—with those hoodlums. But I'll be damned if I thought it was possible . . .

They don't even have any consideration for the dead—the garden of death—damn it all . . . The devil take me, even on the benches they won't leave you in peace."

Huus could have hit him.

They walked through the streets. The tents were closed and deserted. Here and there a merchant was gathering up his wares by the light of a lone lantern.

The noise from the tavern reached out into the street. Sleepy and stooping, people were drifting home two by two.

Marie came into view in the entryway to the hotel. She was drooping and heavy with sleep.

Katinka waited next to the wagon. All around her, wagons were being hitched up and driven off. The Nightingales were singing loudly out in the courtyard.

They climbed into the wagon. Bai wanted to drive and sat next to Marie.

> Oh you—my Valdemar!
> I love you so . . .

"They're still at it," said Bai.

They drove through the night, past the woods, across the flat fields.

Marie sat slumped over the basket in her lap, sleeping. Huus and Katinka sat in silence, gazing out over the landscape. Now and then Bai would speak.

"Hoho, my horses . . . All right, slowly now . . ."

And then there would be silence like before.

Bai wanted to have "some refreshment" and roused Marie until she found a bottle of port wine.

"Do you want some?" he asked.

"No, thanks," said Huus.

"You're making a big mistake." Bai took the bottle from his mouth. "A stomach needs something for the night chill."

Bai took another gulp. "You learn that on the battlefield," he said.

He began to talk about the Prussians and the war.

"Good-natured people," he said, "taken one at a time—big eaters—real gluttons—but good-hearted—really good-hearted—one at a time—but in the corps . . . the devil take them."

No one answered. Marie dozed off again.

Katinka just wished that he would keep quiet.

"But big eaters," said Bai again.

He started waxing patriotic and talking about old Denmark and a bloody banner. Then he fell into silent reveries when no one replied.

The only sound was the noise of the horses in their traces. Now and then a rooster crowed across the fields.

"Put your shawl on," said Huus, "it's cold."

Carefully he placed the blue shawl around Katinka's shoulders.

Little by little the day dawned over the fields.

"We can give you breakfast, can't we?" said Bai. They were home and stood sleepily on the steps in the gray morning.

"Yes, if you like," said Katinka.

But Huus had to go home. It was high time.

"Well . . ." said Bai, "it's up to you." He yawned and went inside. Marie had gone off, lugging the baskets.

Huus and Katinka remained, alone. She leaned against the doorpost. They were silent for a moment.

"Well, thank you for today," she said. It came out gentle and uncertain.

"As if I weren't the one who should thank you." It came out like an explosion, and in a flash Huus grabbed her hand and kissed it twice, three times, with hot lips.

And was up in the wagon and gone.

"What the devil got into him?" asked Bai, coming out. "Is he gone?"

Katinka stood in the same spot. "Yes," she said, "he drove off."

She leaned on the door and went quietly inside.

Katinka was sitting by the open window. The day had burst forth. Larks and all the birds were exulting across the wide meadow. The air was full of song and sunshine and bird trills over the summery fields.

Chapter Four

The watchdog was sleeping in the hot courtyard and refused to be disturbed. A couple of scrubbed basins had been placed in the sun to dry.

Katinka opened the hall door; only the buzz of the flies could be heard throughout the bright, cool rooms.

She walked through the conservatory out to the garden. Not a soul was there and it was completely quiet. Croquet mallets and balls lay abandoned on the croquet field. The rosebushes were drooping in the heat.

"Is that you, dear Mrs. Bai?" Mrs. Linde said softly from the gazebo and nodded. "Yes, Linde is practicing his sermon. They're all out in the back yard—the Kiærs came over, a whole wagonload with their visitors... And it's so inconvenient when Linde is practicing his sermon ..."

"Are the Kiærs here?" asked Katinka.

"Yes... they came over for coffee—they're in the back yard—and the new doctor too... And you've been to the fair... Huus told us about it."

"Yes—it was a lovely day," said Katinka. She had difficulty getting the words out, her heart was pounding so hard.

Old Pastor Linde appeared in the doorway to the garden. He had a handkerchief on his head. The handkerchiefs made an appearance every Friday evening when Pastor Linde began practicing his sermon.

"Is it dear Mrs. Katinka?" he asked. "And are you well?"

The old pastor came over to the gazebo door. He wanted to hear about the fair.

Katinka hardly knew what she was saying. As she was talking she suddenly felt an indescribable longing for Huus.

"Yes, he is truly a fine person," said Mrs. Linde when Katinka had been speaking for a while; and Katinka blushed bright red.

"Yes," said the old pastor, "a nice person."

He took off the handkerchief and placed it on the gazebo table in front of him. He kept on asking questions about the fair. "Our people came home toward morning," he said. "They have to have fun once in a while . . ."

The old pastor chatters away, and Katinka answers without comprehending a word.

"Little Linde—your sermon . . ."

"Yes, little Mother. Well, dear lady," he says, "it's already Saturday today."

Old Pastor Linde shuffles off with his handkerchief in his hand.

"Don't you want to join the others, dear Mrs. Bai?" says Mrs. Linde.

"Unless I can help . . . with anything . . ."

"No, thank you. I'm just going to serve what I have . . . a little ham and peas."

Katinka stood up.

"Go through the courtyard," said Mrs. Linde.

Katinka had not seen Huus for three days, since the fair; how she had hoped and waited, and feared what she hoped for. Now she was going to see him.

Laughter and noise could be heard from the back yard and far out across the field. Katinka opened the gate and went in.

"The lovely woman is coming," shouted Agnes. They were playing "widow" on the big lawn.

Katinka noticed only Huus. He was standing there in the middle of the group. How pale he was and how sad he looked.

Katinka thought: he has been unable to sleep, just as I

have. And she smiled timidly at him, with her head slightly bowed, like a young girl.

She got Agnes and they wound up standing in front of Huus.

"Oh, phooey," said Agnes to Huus, "we know the story: you've had a hangover, of course. That's why you've been invisible for three days. And we've been expecting you. Yesterday Mrs. Bai wouldn't even let us have coffee because we had to wait for you."

Katinka looked down at the ground, but she didn't stop Agnes. It seemed to her that she herself was telling him how she had waited for him.

"And is that any way to behave when you're supposed to be the godfather to a pair of genuine pouter doves?" said Agnes.

The other two didn't say a word. But Katinka felt Huus's eyes on her, and she just stood there in front of him with her head bowed.

They continued to play "troll and widow." She only had eyes for him. They exchanged only the words of the game in low voices. Neither one of them would have been able to speak any louder.

Katinka wasn't aware that during the game her hands lingered in his and released them reluctantly.

Tables were to be set for the evening in the gazebo. Old Pastor Linde and Curate Andersen arrived with Big Louise and Little Miss Jensen.

"Well," said Agnes, "so we finally get a whiff of the ham."

Before they sat down to eat, Big Louise had already skipped in front of the new doctor to show off her "beauty."

When everybody had found a seat in the gazebo, old Linde shouted from the doorway: "Haven't we forgotten a couple on the love bench?"

"The love bench" was an old moldering bench between two trees down by the pond.

"It's so nice and dark," said Mrs. Linde. "In the old days, when our sons were courting, there was always a couple coming back from down there—I mean, each taking a different path here to the gazebo. Yes, those were the days . . ."

"The love bench" was Mrs. Linde's favorite topic.

"Yes, yes, Linde, quite a few have been happy there," she said.

She began counting all those who had become engaged in the parsonage garden. That one, and that one, and . . . There was a merry chatter around the whole table about all the engagements and people falling in love.

"Yes—that summer when both Rikard and Hans Beck got engaged."

"Agnes knew about it, she always rattled the lock before opening the door."

"And the hazelnut promenade . . ."

"Well, yes, you *could* be interrupted . . ."

"Something was always rustling off between the branches."

"Miss Horten had a bright yellow skirt . . . how it *shone*."

"Yes," says the old pastor, "you have to watch out for those bright colors."

"But it's lovely in the hazelnut promenade," blurts out a young girl.

And they all laugh so much that they collapse over the table.

"Linde, Linde," shouts Mrs. Linde, "remember that it's Saturday." The old pastor laughs so hard that he starts to cough.

"But it really was as though you could hear an endless kissing in all the nooks."

"Yes, yes," says Mrs. Linde, who takes a practical view, "they've all gotten on very well."

"*Skaal*, dear Mrs. Katinka, shall we drink a toast, we old people?" says the pastor.

Katinka gave a start. "Thank you . . ."

A young couple was discussed, the latest from the love bench. They already had a son.

"Was it a boy they had?"

"Yes, a wonderful boy."

"He weighed eight pounds," said Mrs. Linde.

"And what a home they have."

"As if cleaned by the wind . . ."

"And such cooing—you'd almost think it was still their honeymoon."

They had finished eating, and Mrs. Linde signaled to the pastor.

"Yes, well," says old Pastor Linde, "how about a toast to Mother?"

"Thank you for dinner."

Everybody stood up and there was a murmuring out in the garden. Katinka leaned against the wall. The noise and conversation out there seemed so far away, and she saw only Huus's pale, emotional face, his beloved face.

A couple of maids came to clear off the table, and Katinka went out into the garden. They were going to play hide-and-seek. Agnes was in the midst of "a thousand and nine, a thousand and ten . . ."

The old pastor said good night. "It's Saturday, you know," he said. He met Bai up by the gate: "Good evening, Stationmaster. Yes, I must be getting to my sermon."

Big Louise was standing next to the large jasmine bush. Everyone was rushing and hiding behind all the shrubs.

"She's peeking, she's peeking," shouted someone as he flew past the jasmine bush.

And then there was silence.

"Here I come!"

Katinka went into the gazebo. She closed the door behind her: she was so tired. And all the words at the dinner table seemed to have wrapped around her like a great, helpless ache.

She was sitting quietly like that when the door opened and shut.

"Huus..."

"Katinka—oh, Katinka..." It sounded despairing and full of tears; and he *pulled* her hands toward him and kissed them again and again as he knelt at her feet.

"Yes, my friend—yes, my friend."

Katinka loosened his hands and leaned for a moment on his shoulder as he knelt there: "Yes, Huus, yes."

Tears ran down her cheeks. With indescribable tenderness she let her hand glide through the hair of the sobbing man.

"Oh—dear Huus—time will soften this... you... When you"—she took her hands away from his hair and leaned against the table—"go away... and we don't see each other anymore..."

"Not see each other anymore?"

"Yes—Huus—that's the way it *has* to be. But I will always remember you—forever and ever..."

She spoke so gently, with thousands of sad caresses in her voice.

"Katinka," said Huus, and lifted his face, bathed in tears.

Katinka gazed down at his face; how she loved every feature. His eyes, his mouth, his brow—which she would never see again, never be near him again.

She took a step as if to go. Then she turned to Huus, who was standing by the table.

"Kiss me," she said and lay her head against his chest.

He took her head in his hands, whispering her name over and over through his kisses.

Out in the garden they were running and scurrying about. Big Louise dashed down the hazelnut promenade after the new doctor and almost knocked over Bai and Kiær in the passageway.

"Yes—we were at the fair," said Bai, "wonderful day... saw a couple of saucy girls in the woods—pretty girls in boots... A veritable breath of fresh air, old Kiær."

"That's what Huus said," says Kiær.

"Huus," Bai stops and speaks in a low voice, "Huus—what did I tell you? Oh, that man doesn't know a damn thing about women. He sat there as embarrassed as a plucked chicken watching the 'Nightingales'... a real pity to look at, old Kiær—a real pity for a well-proportioned man."

Big Louise fell into the new doctor's arms up in front of the jasmine bush.

It was starting to get dark. People were drifting around in the garden, two by two. A name was shouted down the passageway: "All right," came the reply from the meadow by the pond.

And then, as the sabbath bells rang, everything grew quieter. Silently they gathered on the great grass embankment, speaking laconically in low voices.

Katinka sat next to Agnes. The pastor's daughter was always coddling the "lovely woman."

"Sing a little, Miss Emma," said Agnes.

A small woman began to sing as they sat around on the grass embankment. It was the song about Mr. Peder who cast the runes over the bridge. All the girls joined in the chorus.

Agnes gently rocked the lovely woman back and forth as she sang:

> Fair words
> Create my joy so brief
> Fair words
> Often make us weep
> Fair words.

And then it was quiet again.

They sang song after song, first one voice, then more would join in.

Katinka kept sitting next to Agnes, silently leaning against her.

"Sing along, lovely woman," said Agnes, bending her face down toward Katinka.

It had turned completely dark. The shrubs around them were like great silhouettes. And after the hot day the air was fresh with dew and filled with fragrances.

A gentleman spoke to Huus, and he replied. Katinka heard his voice.

" 'Marianna' is so beautiful," said Miss Emma.

"Yes, sing 'Marianna.' "

"Don't get up," Agnes said to Katinka. And then she and Miss Emma sang:

> Beneath the turf of the grave sleeps
>   Poor Marianna—
> The girls come and they weep
>   for poor Marianna.
> Around her heart the serpent writhed,
> Peace no more on earth would thrive,
>   Poor Marianna . . .

"Is the lovely woman cold?"

"We should be getting home," said Katinka.

She stood up. "It's probably quite late," she said.

They were outside the garden. She had said goodbye to him.

She had seen his face, sorrowful and pale, as he hastily bent over her. She had felt the pressure of his hand, clutching so it hurt, and she heard Bai say:

"Bye, Huus, we'll be seeing you."

And quickly, while she forced herself to laugh at something that she had not heard, she shook hands all around; and Agnes put her arm around Katinka's waist and ran up to the garden gate with her.

It banged twice and then fell shut.

And behind them they were singing.

"Let's go this way," she said. It was a path across the fields, along the parsonage garden; they had to walk single file.

Katinka walked slowly behind Bai.

"Good night," they heard. Old Linde had come up onto his little hill. He was wearing his handkerchief.

"Good night, Pastor."

"Good night."

They walked on across the field. With the pastor's "Good night," the tears had suddenly spilled from Katinka's eyes, and she kept on crying silently. She turned around twice and looked back toward Linde standing on his little hill.

"Are you coming?" said Bai.

They reached the house.

And Bai attended to the track and puttered around, chatting, and went to bed; and she went about doing all of the everyday things: covered the furniture and watered the flowers and locked up.

All of it seemed to be behind a veil, in a dream.

She got up the next day and got busy with all the usual things; the 10 o'clock train came and went and she sat at the window in front of the fields that were lying there just like yesterday.

She spoke and was asked everyday questions and gave everyday answers. She was out in the kitchen to help Marie.

The windows and doors stood open. From over at the church the bells began to ring.

Marie was in the middle of a long monologue when her mistress said:

"I'm going to church."

And she was gone before Marie could answer.

It was almost as though her mistress *ran* across the sun-hot fields.

Chapter Five

A few days later Katinka went "home."
One of her brothers had a grocery store in her home town; she stayed with him. Her other brothers had been scattered by the winds.

Her sister-in-law was a kind little woman who brought a child into the world every year and rolled around half embarrassed and cowed in her perpetual pregnancy. She had grown very lazy and somewhat stupid. She couldn't manage to do much else than give birth and nurse.

In their house there was always one room where they hadn't gotten around to putting up the drapes. They lay there newly starched and waiting, spread out over all the chairs. There was always washing going on for the many little children; there were clotheslines everywhere full of linen and socks. The food for their meals was never ready on time, and there were never enough plates when they finally sat down at the table.

"Little Mi and Mother will eat together," said the little woman.

The doors banged constantly and every half hour a screech could be heard through the house, as if from a stuck pig. It was one of the little children who had fallen down somewhere in one of the corners. They always had bruises both front and back.

"Oh, no," said Katinka's brother, "not again . . ."

"Well, what should I do, Kristoffer," said the little woman.

She always said "Well, what should I do, Kristoffer" and looked helpless.

Little by little Katinka brought peace to the house. She needed to have something to do, to know that she was useful; and she went about so quietly while everything was attended to.

The little sister-in-law sat there, as if relieved, and smiled gratefully from her chair in the corner—she always sat in a corner, behind a desk, or next to the sofa—with her timid smile.

Katinka preferred to stay home, indoors. Here was the old furniture from home and all the old things: her father's masterpiece, the oak cupboard with the carved figures on the doors—at home it had stood in the good parlor right between the windows.

"That's Moses and his prophets," her father would say. Katinka thought that "those men" were the most wonderful in the world.

And the marble table which had been bought at an auction and where the "fine things" stood in symmetrical rows: the silver sugar bowl with the coffee pot and the silver goblet that was an award from the guild.

As she went around straightening up the house, Katinka constantly discovered mementos from home: an old cup with an inscription, a yellowing drawing, three or four plates . . .

The old plates with the blue Chinamen and the garden with the three trees and the little bridge over the stream . . . How many stories they had told each other about those Chinamen, at home on Sundays when they used the good dishes.

Katinka asked if she could keep the old plates.

"Of course you may!" said the little woman. "Oh, God— they're all chipped" (everything was chipped in that house)— "everything gets ruined here . . . but what am I to do?"

Katinka preferred to stay inside, or to walk up to the cemetery to the grave. It was best up there. She often felt as if she were a widow who was sitting there next to her husband's grave.

He had died so soon, they had lived together so briefly, and now she was alone, all alone.

While she sat there she would read the inscription on the tombstone: her father's and her mother's names.

Had they loved each other? Her father who always grumbled and sat there and was waited on—and her mother, who had become so different after he died, as if she suddenly blossomed again . . .

She had known so *little* about her parents.

Yes, and they had known so little about each other—everyone who lived and went around close to each other . . .

Katinka leaned her head against the trunk of the weeping willow tree. She felt a bitter sadness that she had never known before.

She was seldom in the town or on the streets. There were so many new things everywhere, and everything was different than before. All new faces and new names and people she didn't know.

She had been out to the old farm. Back rooms had been built in their old workshop. And windows had been put in, along with new doors; and an attic room had been built in their old dovecote.

Katinka didn't go out to the old farm anymore.

She had met Thora Berg on the street.

"But, it's—yes, it's the same old voice—it's Katinka."

"Yes."

"But, child—where have you come from? And you look just the same."

"You do too," said Katinka; she had tears in her eyes.

"I—good gracious—I live here, you know—since last spring—we were transferred. Yes, my dear—there's been a lot of water under the bridge . . . You don't have any children, do you?"

"No."

"I thought so. You can thank God, my dear—I have four... and five boarders... Yes—the salary of a second captain doesn't stretch very far. But you... Where do you two children live? Still at the old place? Oh God—those of us in the military never have a permanent home."

Thora kept on talking. Katinka walked at her side and looked at her. In reality it was the same face; but it was as if all her features had been tightened, and her face looked yellow and sharp in the chin.

"You're looking at me, my dear," said Thora. "Yes, life isn't all club dances, you know..."

She said that she wanted to visit Katinka and take her home to her nest.

"But it's time to prepare for exams, and we're up to our necks in French vocabulary."

They parted. Katinka kept standing there and watched her go. Thora was wearing a short, skimpy velvet jacket and a yellow dress. They were both cut on the bias and seemed to be a little too tight.

They didn't see each other again until about a week later in church.

"Do I ever get out? Yes—every day I've wanted to come see you," said Thora. "Come over and visit us on Wednesday... Wednesday at 3 o'clock... We have the most peace on Wednesdays," she said.

Katinka went over on Wednesday.

Thora was in the kitchen when she arrived, and Katinka waited in the parlor. The room was too big for the furniture, the old furniture from Thora's dowry that had become worn and faded: the furniture stood there and seemed to be stretching to reach each other along the walls. By the window stood a modern flowerpot holder with a rubber plant in it and a rattan chaise longue with an embroidered cover. That was the good furniture.

On the table lay several faded volumes of poetry and a couple of Rhine landscapes, mementos from Thora and the Captain's wedding trip.

On the high, yellow-papered walls hung a few paintings of flowers in narrow gilded frames. They were roses and pansies with great drops of dew that looked like glass beads sprinkled over the petals. Katinka recognized them; Thora had painted them as a girl.

"Yes, using the old talents for decoration, you see," said Thora. She came in as Katinka was looking up at the roses with the glass beads.

The Captain, in a muslin coat and collar, opened the door. "Isn't it time to eat?" he asked.

"We have company, Dahl," said Thora. And the door closed. "Dahl is drawing maps," she said.

The Captain came into view again in a uniform coat with braiding. "Great pleasure, great pleasure," he said and began to pace back and forth. When the Captain wasn't drawing maps or commanding, he always had a deadline and a lengthy calculation in his head. They were the remnants of his lieutenant days and the honeymoon with the two Rhine landscapes.

Thora sat and talked a great deal. Katinka thought that she had acquired such restless eyes, which first moved to the door and then to Dahl, as she chattered on.

"It's quarter past," said the Captain.

"The boys haven't come," said Thora.

"And so we won't eat," said the Captain. "I must tell you, Mrs. Bai, that it's the boys who are the masters in this house."

Thora said nothing. The Captain sat down on a chair in a corner near the desk. The chair back fell off.

"I can't understand why this chair has never been fixed," he said.

"Yes, Dahl . . ."

"We've been waiting for half a year now, Mrs. Bai," said

the Captain. He bowed slightly toward her. "It's the 'custom' here in this house."

The boys announced themselves by tearing headlong down the attic stairs.

"There they are," said Thora. They went into the dining room. The Captain offered his arm to Katinka; Thora quietly propped up the broken chair-back again so it was leaning against the wall.

"Where have you been?" asked the Captain.

"We've been swimming," said the boys. They had smoked for an hour in a ditch and then stuck their heads in a wash basin.

"Those are mine," said Thora. And by this she meant a nine-year-old boy and three little girls, their hair combed with water.

The Captain ate bicarbonate of soda with his meal, and after every bite he wiped off his Napoleon mustache, which was waxed and well-groomed on his weary face.

The Captain talked about wage conditions with the railway.

The boys were five louts from landed estates who were in secondary school. They called "her four" the "beggar children," and regularly made the nine-year-old wet his pants. They were, by the way, quite good-natured.

They gorged themselves like wolves and said that they were never full except "home on the farm."

The nine-year-old sat with large, wise eyes and looked from the boys to Thora.

"There are chips in the china in honor of the guests," said the Captain; he handed Katinka the cucumber salad in a chipped bowl.

"Oh, that happens so easily, Captain," said Katinka.

One of the boys kept asking under his breath for more potatoes; he had seen that there weren't any more on the platter.

"There are cucumbers," said Thora. "Would Dahl like more . . ."

"But you aren't getting anything yourself," said Katinka. "We already have some."

"Dear Mrs. Bai," said the Captain, "*this* is her pleasure. In this house we know nothing of that thing called peace."

Thora cut up the meat for the youngest of the girls with the plastered-down hair.

"The Captain is in such a good mood today—as you can hear," she said, laughing. "Eh, Captain?"

The Captain was always in that mood.

"What did Gustav get in Geography?"

"Good question," came a bass voice from one of the plates.

"Does Gustav think that his father will be satisfied with that?"

"Father doesn't care," said the bass.

They got up from the table. All the doors in the whole house slammed after the boys.

"Yes, Mrs. Bai," said the Captain, "*this* is Thora's invasion. She's afraid we might have peace and quiet in the house someday."

The Captain went in to his maps. Thora was puttering around with many different kinds of coffee blends behind the coffeepot.

"Can't I help you?" asked Katinka.

"No, thank you, dear."

Thora had red spots on her cheeks and put her fingers to her temples. "It's always a little much at dinner, dear," she said.

"But you let it bother you too much, Thora," said Katinka, who was quite warm herself.

"But when you have this commotion from morning till night, my dear," said Thora.

She couldn't sit in peace at her sewing table. The door was constantly being opened. The boys had sworn that "they didn't want any part of that coffee-klatsch"—and every other minute they dashed up and down the attic stairs to ask about vocabulary.

Thora held her hand to her forehead and went from English to German.

The nine-year-old was "practicing" in the dining room.

"Nikolaj—why do you always have to practice when I have a headache? Stop it now!"

Nikolaj quietly tiptoed away from the piano. Thora always scolded "her own" when she was vexed by the "food gobblers."

Thora sat down in a corner of the sofa and pulled her legs up under her, as she had done so often as a girl.

They talked about people in the town.

"Yes, it's all new families—the old ones are gone."

"Yes, the old ones are gone," said Katinka. She looked at Thora, who had leaned her head against the back of the sofa and closed her eyes. How deeply they had sunk in, those eyes.

"In fact, I don't know any of the old ones except your brother," said Thora.

"Oh, well, yes . . ."

Thora laughed. "God, your poor sister-in-law," she said. "Is she really at it again?"

"Yes, poor thing."

They sat there for a while. Then Thora opened her eyes and said:

"Well, dear—we're all here for procreation."

Thora closed her eyes and the two friends sat in silence.

"Yes, dear," said Thora, "life is strange."

Katinka did not stay for tea. She said that she had promised to be home. She needed to get out in the fresh air and be alone. When she reached the street, she suddenly had the idea that she would visit Frøken for a little while. It was so peaceful in the old lady's house and so unchanged. Katinka turned onto Frøken's street. Tears came to her eyes at the sight of the three green lindens outside her windows. She had sat with a lump in her throat at Thora's too—the whole time.

She went up the little staircase next to the green cellar door and knocked. The smell of roses and summer apples met her when she opened the door.

Frøken was fussing about with rose petals for potpourri spread out on newspaper on the bed.

"And they were there from Holmstrup—all the young girls . . . They wanted to have berries from the tree," she said, "now it's almost over . . ."

Katinka had to go out to see the tree and "my roses."

"There were just three roses for Madam Bustrøm's wreath —yes—there were . . . There were three roses, all right . . ."

They went back inside. Frøken went in and out of the room, muttering, so that her words were lost between the doors. Katinka sat on the dais; now and then she simply said yes or no. Through the open kitchen door you could see out into the green garden; the birds were chirping so they could be heard inside.

How quiet it was here, as if there were no other world.

Katinka looked at the old pictures, yellowing in their crooked frames, and she remembered every one. The silver coffeepot on the table, the prize coffee service with its three pairs of cups; and on the sideboard in front of the cloudy mirror, the precious knickknacks covered with draped handkerchiefs; and the runners on the floor leading to all of the doorways; and the cats that circled around on their pillows.

She knew it all.

Frøken kept on chattering and walking in and out. Katinka wasn't listening anymore. It began to grow dark inside, in the shade of the lindens, and the old nooks lay in shadow.

It was the second time that Frøken had mentioned Huus's name out in the kitchen. Katinka gave a start. She thought that she herself had said it aloud, in her thoughts.

"There's a Mr. Huus in your neighborhood," repeated Frøken.

"Yes, Foreman Huus," said Katinka. "Do you know him?"

Frøken appeared in the doorway. Did she know him! He was none other than the second cousin of Cousin Karl at Kærsholm.

The people at Kærsholm, who had married Lundgaards for two generations.

And she began to talk about Huus and about his mother, who was a Lundgaard—of the Lundgaards from the island of Falster—and about their farm and about his ancestors and about Cousin Karl at Kærsholm and about the whole family, as she walked back and forth.

She lit candles in the kitchen and she puttered with the roses on the bed in the bedroom. Katinka sat quietly in her corner and heard only *his* name, which came up again and again.

It was the first time she had heard his name in all these weeks.

"But how *is* he?" said Frøken. She came in and lifted the cat sleeping in the armchair and sat down by the dais with her hands folded over the cat in her lap.

Katinka began to talk—a few ordinary words, hesitantly, and as if she were thinking about something else. But then it *seized* her: to talk about him, to say his name, to be able to mention his name.

And she talked about Christmas and about the blue shawl and New Year's Eve when he came in the sleigh, and the winter nights when they kept him company on the road beneath all those stars . . .

"Yes," said Frøken from her chair, "yes, they're nice people . . . those Huuses."

Katinka kept on talking in a low voice from her corner in the shadow.

When spring came, how he had helped her in the garden; he had planted roses; he could do anything . . .

"Yes," said Frøken, "they're a nice family."

And the summer days—and the fair . . . she told her about everything.

Frøken had begun to nod in her chair—Frøken would easily grow sleepy whenever she had to *listen*—and soon she was asleep with her hands folded over her cat.

Katinka stopped and sat in silence. Outside the gaslights were lit, and they illuminated the parlor: the pictures on the wall, the old clock, and Frøken, who was sleeping with her cat on her lap and her head down on her breast.

Frøken woke up and raised her head.

"Yes," she said, "he's a nice person."

Katinka didn't hear what she said. She simply got up to leave and get away. And outside in the fresh air, along the roads behind the town where she walked, her longing only seemed to grow with every single step.

A few days later she received a letter from Bai in the morning post. The strangest thing that has happened here, he wrote, has to do with Huus. Last week he left for Copenhagen on business, he said. And then several days later he wrote to Kiær—can you imagine?—asking him to release him from his position. He had gotten the chance to travel to Holland and Belgium, he wrote—on a stipend, can you imagine, and would send a replacement, and that replacement arrived yesterday. Kiær is cursing and I was sorry about it too, now that we had gotten so used to that wet blanket.

The letter lay open on the table in front of Katinka. And she had read it over and over. She hadn't realized that she had still been hoping. But she *had* thought that it was all a dream: a *miracle* had to happen. But she *had* to see him again, and he would not leave.

But now he *had* left. Left and gone away.

Her brother's children were jabbering around her, having their bowls of bread and milk.

"Aunt, Aunt Tik!"

The second youngest fell off his chair and howled.

"Jesus, did little Emil fall?" said the little woman.

Katinka lifted Emil up and dried his face, and without realizing it herself, she turned back to her letter.

Left and gone away.

But now she wanted to go *home,* to be in her own house and not among these strangers.

At any rate, she wanted to go home.

It was her last afternoon there. The nursemaid had gone off to the grove with the flock of children.

Katinka and her sister-in-law were sitting alone in the parlor. Her sister-in-law was brooding over the children's clothes.

Then, as they sat there, the little woman suddenly put her head down on her sewing box and sobbed.

"But Marie," said Katinka, "my dear Marie . . ."

She got up and went over to her sister-in-law. "What is it, Marie?" she said.

The little woman continued to sob into her sewing box.

Katinka took her head in her hands and spoke softly to her. "But Marie—dear Marie . . ."

The little woman looked up. "Yes," she said, "now you're going away . . . And you were so good to me . . ." She sobbed and again put her head down on her sewing box. "So good to me . . . me, who is always stuck in the middle of all this . . . Always . . ."

Katinka was touched; she knelt down on the floor in front of the little woman and took her hands. "But Marie," she said, "things will change, you know."

"Yes," and the little woman kept on crying with her head bowed, "when I'm old one day, or when I die."

Katinka pulled her sister-in-law's hands away from her face, and was going to speak.

But then she saw her sister-in-law's childlike face, wet with tears, and her poor little deformed figure; silently she went back to her place while the little woman kept on crying.

In the evening Katinka went up to the cemetery. She
wanted to say goodbye to her parents' grave.

She met Thora. She had brought a wreath for her mother's
grave; it was her birthday.

The two friends stood together in front of the grave.

"Yes, dear," said Thora, "someday we'll all be lying here
with our noses in the air."

They parted at the grave of Katinka's parents.

"People always meet each other again in this world," said
Thora.

Katinka went over to the grave and sat down on a bench
beneath the willow. She gazed at the dead stone with its
inscription, and she felt that she had lost everything in the
world—including her childhood home.

What had become of it all? Gray and tormented and so
miserable—everything.

She saw Thora before her with her restless eyes and she
heard the Captain: "There are chips in the china in honor of
the guests . . ." And she saw her little sister-in-law's face when
she had cried.

And here—this spot with the dead stone and the two names
—this was now the entire memory of her youth and her home.

She sat there for a long time. And she gazed into the life
she would now lead, and it seemed to close around her, all of
it, a single, unimaginable, drenching hopelessness.

She stepped out of the train car, down onto the platform,
and she allowed herself to be kissed by Bai, and Marie took
her things, and she had only one thought: to get inside the
house—inside.

It seemed to her that Huus had to be inside, waiting.

And she went on ahead and opened the door to the parlor
which was waiting, clean and nice; to the bedroom; to the
kitchen where everything shone; clean and—empty.

"My God, how thin the mistress has become," began Marie, who was lugging the bags.

And then she really got started, while Katinka, pale and tired, collapsed into a chair—about the whole area. About what had been happening and what was being said. Over at the inn they had had summer guests who came with bedsteads and everything, and at the parsonage there were visitors right up to the rafters.

And Huus, who had left . . . all of a sudden . . .

"Well, I thought so . . . Because he was down here on that last evening . . . and it seemed to me just like he was going around saying goodbye to everything—he sat in the parlor alone—and out in the garden . . . and out here on the steps with the doves."

"*When* did he leave?" asked Katinka.

"It must be about two weeks ago."

"Two weeks . . ."

Katinka calmly got up and went out into the garden. She walked along the pathway, over to the roses, down to the elder tree. He had been here to say goodbye to her—at every spot, in every place. She had no tears. She felt almost a quiet solemnity.

There was a happy shout out on the road. She heard Agnes's voice in the midst of a great chorus. She practically jumped up. She didn't want to see them here just now.

Agnes rushed at her like a big dog to welcome her, so that she almost fell over; and the entire party from the parsonage came in for hot chocolate, and a table was set in the garden beneath the elder, and they all stayed until the 8 o'clock train.

The train roared off, and they were gone again—you could hear them talking noisily along the road. Peter, the station hand, had taken the milk cans away, and Katinka was sitting alone on the platform.

"Oh yes," said Bai from the window, "I have greetings for you from Huus."

"Thank you."

"Hm, how short the days are getting... And there's a devil of a cold wind. You ought to come in, you know."

"Yes, I'm coming."

Bai shut the window.

The noise of the parsonage guests died away. Everything was quiet and desolate.

Katinka remained sitting in front of the silent fields in the twilight. This is where she would live now.

Little Ida had written about it in all her letters for the past month. But Mrs. Abel didn't dare hope. Her Little Ida was so sanguine.

Now she was sitting on the wet dishrag next to the stove with the letter in her hand, bawling.

Big Louise had gone for a walk to look for mushrooms near the doctor's house. When she came home, the widow was still in her kitchen chair, rocking.

"What is it?" asked Big Louise; she thought her mother was sitting there looking so strange.

"Ida, my youngest," the widow began to howl.

"Nonsense," said Big Louise. Her mother handed her the letter with a gesture like the heroic mothers in tragedies.

Big Louise read it cold-heartedly. "That's nice," she said, "for her. She's had a whole summer, after all."

Big Louise went in and pounded on the piano. Then, as she sat there, she too howled with her head bent over the keys.

"You must congratulate her," she said suddenly in the midst of her sobs.

"What did you say?"

"I said, you do have to congratulate her," said Big Louise, drying her eyes. She began to resign herself to the new situation.

"Yes, my dear," said the widow dully.

"I can take the message down. I'll stop by the parsonage. You can go over to Jensen's and the miller's..." Big Louise arranged the procession. She realized that she was the *sister-in-law*, at any rate.

She behaved like a child and shouted "Long live the postal service" as she ran off from the station, swinging her parasol.

He was with the postal service.

The widow went happily from Jensen's to the miller's and wept that she was going to lose her dove.

"Joakim Barner—of the aristocratic Barners," said the widow. "He's employed in the postal service."

At the parsonage the widow met up with her eldest.

"Yes, I felt the need to tell our spiritual advisor myself." Mrs. Abel used her handkerchief again. "On such solemn occasions," she said.

The old pastor patted his stomach with satisfaction. The strawberry liqueur was set on the table along with cookies. Mrs. Linde sat on the sofa with Mrs. Abel to find out how it had "happened." It had "happened" in a gazebo... near the shore.

The old pastor drank a toast with Big Louise.

"Well, well, you know how it goes as soon as the bottle's opened... Things get *moving*," said the old pastor.

"Pastor, the thought of losing both of them—my last one..." The widow had a fit of anxious tenderness toward her last one.

The last one was as affectionate as a young filly in honor of the day.

"So she *still* has a chance to turn out quite nice," said Mrs. Linde, stacking up the cookie plates after they had left. "There's a good foundation in them, Linde."

"Heaven knows what Agnes will say..."

Agnes was in the woods with some young people.

"Well, thank God," she said when she came home and heard about it.

"God have mercy, they're crushing that little man," said Agnes. She was standing at the platform gate and watching the Abel family, who had come to get the son-in-law.

The little man flew from one member of the Abel family to another, as helpless as a bean in a grinder.

"Well," said Agnes, "you can see he's got water on the brain."

She put her arm around Katinka's waist and they went into the garden.

"Yes," she said, closing the gate, "*now* they're happy."

They sat down under the elder tree. Suddenly Agnes said: "I'm going away now... next week. I've told them at home. The situation here is impossible to endure." Agnes tore to shreds the leaves that had fallen on the table. "It has to come to an end sometime."

Katinka sat and stared into space. "Agnes, do you believe that people can run away from their sorrows?" she said softly.

"I'll have work too... the schoolteacher exam. There's nothing else. Because sitting behind a glass window in a post office isn't much fun... and it's too late for anything serious."

Katinka nodded. "Yes," she said, "that's right."

"Hm," said Agnes, "we women don't really have very many opportunities; the first twenty-five years of our life we dance around waiting to get married—and the last twenty-five we sit around waiting to be buried."

Agnes leaned her elbows on the table and supported her head with her hands.

"Lovely," she said to herself.

Suddenly she put her hands over her face and burst into tears.

"And oh, how I'll miss him," she said.

She wept for a long time with her face in her hands. Then she let her arms fall to the table. She looked at Katinka; the lovely woman sat leaning forward with her hands in her lap; tears were rolling slowly down her cheeks.

"How good you are," said Agnes, bending toward her. "Lovely woman . . ."

The following week Agnes Linde left.

The Abel family was a virtual dovecote. They made themselves understood with affectionate sibilant sounds and little squeals.

"He calls me Missy Mother," said the widow. "Yes, he makes up names for us."

When strangers were present, the engaged couple would drape themselves dully over a couple of chairs until one of them said "Busse-Bisse" and they would disappear behind closed doors.

"That's their language," said the widow. Their language was a little difficult for strangers.

When the guests were about to leave, "Basse" and "Bosse" had to be called for ten minutes. "They're probably in the garden," said the widow. Basse and Bosse were constantly in the garden; they would hide any place there was a little dense vegetation.

When Basse and Bosse appeared, they looked flustered and bright red.

Big Louise and the little man thrived on minor skirmishes with wrestling holds. The little man gave her "brother-in-law kisses" and tickled her behind doors.

At parties they were all sleepy and sat in the corner. At dinner the widow would make sugary little *busse-busse* sounds toward "her three." She herself didn't know what it meant.

If they were home in the evening, the lamp was not lit.

"We're having twilight time," said the widow, "all of us."

The little man would sit between Bosse and Lisse-Sa on the sofa. Miss Jensen and the widow would say something into the dusk once in a while. There would be a slight creaking from the sofa. They would sit like that for hours.

When Miss Jensen went over to her own place, she would kiss Bel-Ami on his cold snout.

Sometimes Basse and Bosse would go down across the fields to the evening train. They would walk up and down the platform and gaze into each other's eyes; when they turned around, the little man would kiss Bosse-Sa on her ear.

Katinka sat on the platform bench with Huus's blue shawl around her. When the train was gone, she could hear the engaged couple dallying home on the path through the field.

Katinka got up and went inside. The days were growing short; they already had to have light at teatime.

"The lamp, Marie," she said.

Marie came in and stood with the lamp next to the piano. The light fell on Katinka's narrow little face and her white, transparent hands which remained resting on the last keys.

"Call Bai for tea," said Katinka. She leaned on the piano to get up from her chair. She was always so tired, as if there were lead in her legs.

They drank tea and Bai read the newspapers with his toddy.

Katinka took a book out of the bag. It was always the "new" books: Agnes and Andersen had always fought over them.

The book lay open under the lamp. Katinka never got any farther into it than twenty pages: it wasn't life, after all, and not even real poetry that could take your thoughts away.

She took out her poetry album; she had written "Marianna" in it with a date. And when she put the album down again, she stood in front of the drawer for a moment before she shut it. The little Japanese tray lay wrapped in the yellowing bridal veil.

She went out into the kitchen too. She had her favorite place on the chopping block in the corner. Marie was sewing in front of a candle on the table and chattering away. She was a faithful soul who didn't forget her old love.

She still talked about Huus and how lonely it had become.

Katinka sat silently in the corner. Once in a while she would shake as if she were cold, and she would press her arms tightly against her breast.

Marie kept on talking with her big red face close to the lone candle.

"We ought to go to bed," said Bai, opening the door.

"Yes, Bai . . ."

"Good night, Marie."

Autumn arrived with melancholy veils of fog over the fields. The sky lay low over the days, which slunk from night to night in the dusk.

"You have to pull yourself together, dear Mrs. Bai," said the young doctor. "You've got to build up your strength."

"Yes, Doctor."

"And *walk*. You must get some exercise. Your strength is quite gone."

"Yes, Doctor, I'll go for walks."

"Anything else new?" The doctor got up. "Have you had a letter from Miss Agnes?"

"Yes—a while ago."

"They say that Andersen is thinking of leaving."

"I heard that," said Katinka. "Everyone goes away from here . . ."

"Oh, no, dear Mrs. Bai, there are some who stay too."

"Yes, *we* stay, Doctor."

"Your wife isn't doing very well," the doctor says out in the office, where he lights a cigar.

"No, it's a hell of a mess," says Bai.

"She doesn't have any strength . . . Well, good morning, Stationmaster."

"Yes, damn it all . . . Well, morning, Doctor."

"You have to *walk*, Tik," said Bai when he came in from the freight train. "You're not doing anything about it."

Katinka walked. She dragged herself across the fields in all kinds of weather.

She walked down to the church. Gasping for breath she rested on the meeting stone outside the church. The cemetery lay flat and flowerless behind the white wall. Only the boxwood hedges stood stiffly around the rigid crosses with their names.

She walked home again—across the meadows. The noon train came roaring over the bridge and curved out of sight. The smoke lay like a darker spot in the gray fog for a moment, and then dispersed.

On the other side of the river they were plowing. The sod was pared up in long furrows behind the steady plow.

Katinka arrived home.

The miller had been there, or the foreman from Kiær's.

"Energetic fellow, that Svendsen," said Bai to Katinka. "Really up on everything, nice fellow."

To Kiær he said, "Can't tell how he is at his job, though."

Kiær grumbled something.

"But he's a lively fellow, one of us, old Kiær."

Svendsen collected Greek cards and pictures in sealed envelopes. He brought them along down to the station, and he and Bai went through them over their toddies. "Let's have a look at the 'archives,' " said Svendsen.

"Fine with me." Bai was always willing.

Svendsen got the "latest ones" from Hamburg C.O.D.

"What damned filth," said Bai happily. He always spoke more quietly whenever they were "in the archives," even though the door was closed.

"What damned filth, old Svendsen," he said, holding the cards up to the lamp.

They kept on looking at the cards. Bai rubbed his knees.

"But this is a good one," he said. "This one's *dangerous*."

Svendsen rubbed his finger under his nose and sniffed.

"Meat," he said, "that's real meat."

They had come to the last of the pictures and sat for a while with their toddy glasses. It was as if Bai had collapsed.

"Yes," he said, "but how is *life*, Svendsen? How is life, old man, with an ailing wife?"

Svendsen did not reply.

Bai sighed and stretched out his legs.

"Yes, old man," he said, "yes—it sure is."

Svendsen had been sitting in philosophical silence. Now he stood up. "No, you never know what was sung at your cradle," he said.

Bai got up and opened the door to the parlor.

"What?" he said. "Are you sitting there in the dark?"

"Yes." Katinka stood up in the corner. "I was sitting here for a moment in the dark. Did you want anything, Bai?"

"I'm going part way with Svendsen," said Bai.

Katinka came in to say goodbye.

"Mrs. Bai is still rather peaked," said Svendsen, feeling his pockets to see whether he had his collections.

Bai was ready and they said goodbye.

"Good God—Mrs. Bai ought to stay inside—it's much too cold."

"I'll just go with you to the gate," she said.

They went out onto the platform. "The stars are so bright," said Bai.

"That means frost. Good night, Mrs. Bai."

The gate slammed shut.

"Good night."

Katinka stood leaning against the gate. The voices died

away. Katinka raised her head: Yes, the sky was clear, and all the stars up there . . .

As if she wanted to lament her suffering to the dead tree, Katinka bent down and threw her arms around the damp post.

The Lindes came over often in the evening now. They missed Agnes, those two old folks.

And Andersen was going to leave too.

"He wants to leave," said the old pastor. "And now we sit here and risk getting one of those 'living word' types . . ."

Pastor Andersen had gotten a position on the west coast.

Mrs. Linde wept in secret.

"Oh God, I saw it, you know," she said. "I saw it, all right. But they don't know what they want, Mrs. Bai. They don't know what they want, my friend . . . That's youth—a different kind of youth these days, dear Mrs. Bai. They go around asking whether they love each other, and they each go their own way and are unhappy their whole life.

"I read my fortune in the egg whites, my dear, before Linde asked me to marry him, and we have taken the bad with the good for *thirty* years . . .

"But now we'll have Agnes sitting there, a lonely girl, when the two of us old people close our eyes one day."

The men came in. The old pastor had to have his whist.

Katinka felt happiest whenever the old pastor was there. Such peace seemed to follow him.

When he sat there in his skullcap with his few øre, playing well, his old face happy, he would say: "There you see, old man," whenever he took a trick.

The two old people quarreled.

"It's like I told you, Linde . . ."

"If you'll just believe me, my dear . . ." and he spread out his hand.

"Your turn, dear Mrs. Bai, it's your turn."

Katinka was daydreaming. She sat and gazed at the two old people.

"Queen of diamonds. There you see, old man."

They played the last rubber with a dummy. Katinka went around getting things ready for dinner. They were eating better and better at the Bais'. Bai had so many favorite dishes that Katinka made.

Many days she was in the kitchen from early in the morning, boiling and sautéing, following recipes and cookbooks. Difficult creations that demanded scraping and peeling.

Tired, Katinka sat down on the butcher block and coughed.

"The mistress is slaving herself into consumption, just so they can stuff their mouths—that's the way it will end," said Marie.

"Would you like a gin?" asked Katinka.

"If you have some . . ."

When he nodded you could see that Bai had acquired a double chin. He had put on weight in general. With a little coquette bulge under his vest and dimples at his knuckles.

"It's ready now," said Katinka.

"Thank you, dear," said Bai.

Lately there had been something rather sultan-like about Bai. Perhaps it came with the corpulence.

"Thank you, dear, we'll just finish the hand," he repeated.

Katinka sits down on a chair at the table and waits. The old pastor looks at Bai and across the set table to his silent wife. Katinka is leaning her head on her hand.

"All right, Mr. Mayor," says old Linde to Bai.

Katinka gets up. Something was missing from the table. The door closes after her, and the old pastor again looks across the illuminated table and at Bai, who is holding his cards over the coquette bulge.

"Yes, Inspector," says the old pastor, "you're a lucky man in your home."

Afterwards they sit over milk punch and cookies. "It's the good husbands who are fond of sweets," says Mrs. Linde. Bai wants more vanilla wafers from the box.

And they continue to munch around the lamp.

"Won't you play a little?" asks Mrs. Linde.

"Or sing one for us—one of Agnes's," says the old pastor.

Katinka goes over to the piano. And in a faint voice she softly sings the song about Marianna.

The old pastor listens with folded hands and Mrs. Linde lets her knitting drop.

> Beneath the turf of the grave sleeps
> > Poor Marianna—
> The girls come and they weep
> > for poor Marianna.

"Thank you," said the old pastor.

"Thank you, dear Mrs. Bai," said Mrs. Linde.

She couldn't really see the stitches until she had dried her eyes.

Katinka remained sitting with her back to the others. Slowly the tears dropped from her cheeks onto the keys.

"Yes, youth nowadays has a lot of ideas," said the old pastor. He was gazing off into space and thinking about Agnes.

They got up to leave and Mrs. Linde put on her wrap in the bedroom. The two candles in front of the mirror were lit. It was so bright and cheerful with all the whiteness of the bed and the mirror.

"Yes," said Mrs. Linde, "if only we could see Agnes in a home like this." She was still sniffling as she tied her hat ribbons.

"I'll keep the pastor and his wife company," said Bai. "A man needs a little exercise."

"Yes," said the pastor, "a person needs some exercise after that jellied eel.

"You eat too well at the station. Mother has forbidden me to set foot here on Saturdays."

"I won't go any farther," said Katinka and stopped in the doorway. "The doctor wants me to be careful with my cough."

"No, go inside, the fall is the worst time."

"Good night, good night."

Katinka went inside. She took out an old letter from Agnes, crumpled and well perused, and spread it out under the lamp:

"... And so I had hoped that the first days would be the worst, and that time would heal. But the first days were *good* and nothing compared to now. Because then there was a pain in which everything was immediate. But when it dwindles like this, day by day, like earth slipping away, every new morning that awakens us will only distance us more and more. And there is nothing new, Katinka, no shadow of anything new, only all the old things, the memories, which we unravel again and again and huddle over ... Then it's as if a great sucking creature were sitting on your heart. Memories are disastrous for both body and soul."

Katinka leaned back with her head against the cold wall. Her face was so pale in the lamplight. She had no more tears.

Bai came home.

"It's late," he said. "Damn, how time flies ... I dropped in somewhere with Kiær. It was Kiær who was buying ... I ran into him ... on the way home."

"Is it late?" was all Katinka said.

"Yes, it's past one ..." Bai began to get undressed. "Damn, all this keeping folks company ..." he said.

Bai was always keeping people company on their way "home" lately. He would go to the inn. "Well, I ought to be getting back to protect hearth and home," he would say and bid farewell to the guests.

He "protected" it at the inn with a girl who had worn

short puffed sleeves over a pair of soft arms in the summer. It got to be one o'clock and then two while he "protected" it.

"You could come to bed too, you know," he said to Katinka. "You're sitting up in the cold."

"I didn't know it was so late . . ."

The bed creaked in there underneath Bai; he was stretching. Katinka put the flowerpots in a row on the floor. She coughed when she bent down.

"Damned rheumatism," said Bai. "It aches so much."

"I could rub your arms," said Katinka.

It had become an evening ritual for Katinka to rub Bai's arms with a miracle salve against rheumatism.

"Oh, it's all right," said Bai. He turned over a couple of times and fell asleep.

Katinka heard the night train. It roared across the bridge and came in with a clatter—now it had rushed past.

Katinka hid her face in the sheets in order not to wake up Bai with her coughing.

Winter came, and Christmas. Agnes was home, and the "postal service" arrived on Christmas Eve at the Abels'.

Little Jensen and Bel-Ami came to the station just like the year before. Now Bel-Ami was carried around officially.

"He's gone blind," said Little Jensen. The animal was so lazy that he wouldn't even open his eyes.

When the tree was lit, Bai brought a sealed telegram and placed it on Katinka's table.

The telegram was from Huus.

Bai and Little Bentzen were napping in the office. Katinka and Miss Jensen sat in the parlor, where the candles on the tree were burning down.

Little Jensen nodded as she dozed and struck her head on the piano.

Katinka gazed at the darkened tree. Her hand slid gently over Huus's telegram lying in her lap.

Chapter Six

Winter passed and then spring and summer, which smiled over the fields.

"Dreariness, old friend," said Bai to Kiær. "Yesterday I moved up to the attic room. A man has to get his sleep, you know, if he's going to take care of his business during the day."

Katinka's cough echoed through the house.

Marie brought her wine and water and stood by her mistress's bed. It was as though the cough were going to break her apart.

"Thank you, thank you," she said. "Go in and sleep now." She was breathing heavily. "What time is it?"

"Three thirty."

"Oh," Katinka lay back on the bed, "not more than that?"

Marie tiptoed away on bare feet to her sofa, and a little while later her deep breathing could be heard. The spot of light from the night lamp behind the bed was sketched on the silent ceiling. Katinka lay with her eyes closed.

In the morning she was up. She was sitting in blankets out on the platform bench in the sunshine.

The slim conductor with the tight pants was on the noon train. He jumped off and asked after her health.

"You'll see," he said, "the clear fall air . . ."

"Perhaps," said Katinka and gave him her damp, listless hand.

Bai and the conductor walked down the platform.

"Both lungs," said Bai. He had gotten into the habit of wiping his eyes with two fingers.

"It's God's will," he said, sighing.

The train began to move. "Tight Pants" jumped on. He kept on looking back at Katinka, who was sitting there so little and pale in the sunshine.

He was so sorry, really sorry . . .

Yes—it was damned sad.

There had even been a time last winter when he had thought all kinds of things . . . She sat there on the platform so often and looked so wistful . . .

He had drunk a few toddies with Bai on several evenings, but he had gotten out of the habit.

It had just been her illness, which was progressing.

The train swayed off across the meadows. The sky and the plain shone in the bright autumn air.

The starlings clamored along the telegraph wire and gathered in flocks.

"They're leaving now," said Katinka. With her eyes she followed the departing flocks through the clear sky.

The doctor came and sat down beside her. "Well, how are you?"

"I'm sitting here gathering my strength," she said, "for tomorrow."

"For tomorrow?—Oh, that's right, it's the birthday."

"Yes."

"But you'll keep our agreement, dear Mrs. Bai?"

"Yes—as soon as they've eaten, I'll go to bed."

It was Bai's birthday. Katinka wanted him to have his party. She had been talking about it for a long time: she would stay up for dinner; afterwards they would go into Bai's office to play cards anyway—so they wouldn't even notice that she was ill.

"This one day, at least," she said.

"You should go in now," said the doctor.

"All right." Katinka stood up.

"Let me help you."

"Thank you, it's the stairs," she said. "It's always difficult with the stairs."

Her poor heavy feet couldn't go up the three little steps.

"Thank you, Doctor. But my shawl . . ."

The doctor takes the blue shawl from the bench. "Your favorite one," he says.

Katinka turns around in the doorway and looks out over the fields. "It's so beautiful here this time of year," she says.

In the afternoon she put everything for the salads on the parlor table. She cut beets and potatoes into little pieces on a cutting board.

Miss Jensen came to visit. Katinka nodded.

"Yes, I can still do this," she said. "Is there anything new?" She leaned back. Her hands were so tired, and it made her lungs ache when she held up her arms.

"I haven't seen the Abels for such a long time."

"They're hoping that Barner will be hired," says Little Jensen.

"Yes, he did apply."

Little Jensen gets her cup of coffee. "Give me the oil, Marie," says Katinka.

She is given a battery of bottles and large bowls. "How heavy it is," she says; she can hardly lift the big vinegar bottle. She tastes a sample and stirs the bowls.

"No," she says suddenly, pushing them away from her. "No, I can't taste anything anymore."

She sits there, tired, with her eyes closed. Red spots have spread across her cheeks.

"But I could help, you know," says Little Jensen.

"Oh, Marie can do it. I just have to go to bed."

But all afternoon Marie has to bring everything back and forth so she can see it while she's lying down. She raises herself up in bed while her lungs burn. "Yes," she says, "Bai is used to having it that way."

Marie has to take the fine china and glasses and the fine sets of knives and forks into the bedroom and polish and rub them and line them up on the table.

Katinka lies there counting and figuring, her eyes shining with fever.

"I wonder if everything's here," she says.

She lies there for a moment, listlessly, rubbing her dry, hot, feverish face against the pillow.

"The toddy spoons, Marie," she says then. "We've forgotten the toddy spoons."

"We could put them on Huus's tray," says Marie. She comes in with the spoons on the little Japanese tray.

"No, not on that." Katinka raises herself halfway out of bed.

"Give it to me," she says. She takes the tray and holds her burning palms over the cool enamel. Silently she lies there with Huus's tray in her hands.

Bai comes in and looks at all the china and glasses lined up on the table, polished and shiny.

"Foolishness, my dear," he says. "Foolishness—I told you . . . You just lie here getting worse—Tik," he takes her hand, "Yes—you're burning up."

"Oh, it's nothing," says Katinka, quietly pulling her hand from his. "I just hope we aren't missing anything . . ."

Bai starts to count.

"I suppose there will be compote on the table," he says.

"Yes."

"Well, there aren't any bowls."

"Then we've forgotten them."

"Yes, since I can't do it myself, Bai," says Katinka; she sinks back onto the pillows.

The guests were the "old soap cellar," as Bai called them.

"A man feels at home," he said, "with the soap cellar, the agreeable fellows."

The agreeable fellows were three landowners, with Kiær in the lead and Bai as the fourth man.

Svendsen came along as an extra.

"He's *amusing*," said Bai to Katinka. Katinka had never heard Mr. Svendsen be amusing. Whenever she was present, he contented himself with cleaning his nails or chewing on his mustache.

"Bring him along, Kiær," said Bai. "He likes to sit there and lounge as the fifth man."

Katinka opened the door to the office herself. "It's ready, Bai," she said.

The gentlemen came in. Katinka was dressed up, with a high ruff at the neck up to her gaunt little face.

She sat next to Kiær at dinner.

They talked about her illness. Oh, just wait, winter was the best time . . . The still, clear cold—it would bring strength.

"Yes, the still, clear cold."

"Shall we drink to that?" said Bai. They drank. "Drink up," said Bai.

The agreeable fellows ate with their napkins fastened with a pin at the neck. They sniffed at every mouthful of mayonnaise before they savored it.

"Oil," said landowner Mortensen, sniffing.

Katinka sat there with a few little morsels on her plate. She sat quite straight because of the pains in her chest. The fork shook in her hand when she tried to eat. "Take it away, Marie," she said.

The ducks were brought in, and Kiær drank a toast to Bai: "We all know where 'the heart' and the 'fourth man' sits. A toast to him."

They grew livelier and drank individual toasts to each other. They talked about centrifuges and a new livestock tariff.

"Hey, old man—here's to a good year!"

Bai drank again.

Katinka's cheeks were burning and she saw their faces as if through a gray veil. She pressed herself hard against the back of the chair and looked at Bai, who kept on eating.

"It just *lies* there on your tongue—lies on your tongue," Kiær assured her and poured an old vintage burgundy into her glass.

"Thank you, thank you."

Landowner Mortensen wanted to permit himself to empty a glass . . . He stood up and loosened the napkin at his neck: short and sweet, he wanted to empty this glass . . .

Whenever landowner Mortensen emptied a glass he became religious. By the fifth sentence he would inevitably speak of "those who have gone before," who were looking down from their heaven . . .

There was always something looking down on landowner Mortensen from its heaven.

The agreeable fellows sat with noses drooping and stared down at their plates.

Katinka hardly heard him. She was gripping the seat of her chair with her hands and turning pale and flushed.

When Mr. Mortensen was done, he was still able to enjoy another piece of duck.

"Dear Mrs. Bai, your ducks, now *that's* roasting."

Katinka only heard the voices indistinctly, and she leaned on the table when she stood up.

The gentlemen went into the office; Katinka fell back onto her chair. Bai opened the door and came back in.

"It went really well, Tik, marvelous . . . And you held up so well."

Katinka straightened up and smiled. "Yes. Now you will have your toddies."

Bai went in. Katinka remained sitting in front of the abandoned table with the bottles and glasses that were half full.

In the office they were laughing and interrupting each
other in loud voices—you could hear Kiær.

"Take the lamps in there," said Katinka. The salvos of
laughter struck her every time Marie opened the door.

"The mistress should go to bed," said Marie.

"That can wait . . ."

"For the sake of those gluttons." Marie slammed the
kitchen door so that Katinka jumped.

There was only a single candle left in the middle of the
table. It looked so sad in the dusk, that big, littered dinner
table.

Katinka was so tired; she had to sit here for a little while in
the corner until she gathered her strength.

Marie went from the kitchen to the office, slamming the
doors.

How they were amusing themselves in there. That must be
Svendsen singing.

Katinka listened to the voices from her corner and watched
Marie, who went in and out the illuminated doors with glasses
and bottles.

Things would also be this way even after she was gone and
forgotten someday.

"Marie," she said.

She tried to get up and walk, but she held on to the wall
and couldn't. Marie supported her into the bedroom.

"That's what you get for putting on that act," said Marie.

Katinka had a long coughing attack as she sat on the edge
of the bed.

"Close the door," she said.

She kept on coughing. "And Bentzen should have some
dinner," she said.

"Oh, there's plenty of time for him to eat," said Marie.
She took off Katinka's clothes and went about cursing.

Svendsen was singing in there with a thick voice:

> Oh, my Charles—
> Send me a letter please—
> And set my heart at ease . . .

And there was a clinking of glasses. "Quiet!" shouted Kiær. "Quiet—you old-timers . . ."

Katinka had lain there dozing and woke up. It was Bai.

"Well, that was *that* celebration," he said. He was boisterous from all the toddies.

"Have they left?" asked Katinka. "What time is it?"

"About two thirty . . . It gets late when you're together with a group like that . . ."

He sat down next to the bed and chattered on about everything.

"Damn, the stories he knew, that Svendsen—hell of a lot of stories . . ." He told a couple of them and slapped his thighs with laughter.

Katinka lay there burning with fever.

"But it's a pack of lies," said Bai finally.

He had an attack of emotion as he said good night, and in the doorway he told one last story about Mortensen's milkmaid.

"Yes, well, you need rest," he said. "Good night."

"Good night."

The next few days Katinka grew worse. The doctor came a couple of times a day.

"Devil of a mess," said Bai. "And she held up so well, Doctor, on my birthday . . ."

"Yes—but now she *isn't* holding up so well, Mr. Bai," said the doctor.

No one was allowed to visit Katinka. She was to have absolute quiet.

Madam Madsen from the inn had heard *that* before. But you could at least cheer her up, she thought, so she wouldn't lie there rubbing her eyes in the dark.

Madam Madsen came over to the bed.

It was dark with the curtains rolled down. "Who is it?" asked Katinka from her pillows.

"It's me," said Madam Madsen. "Madam Madsen from the inn."

"Hello," said Katinka and stretched out her hand, which was burning.

"Well—so things are that bad?" said Madam Madsen.

"Yes," Katinka turned her head slightly on the pillow, "I'm not feeling very well."

"No . . . I can see that," said Madam Madsen angrily. She sat looking at Katinka's gaunt face in the dark.

"And it's all because of that shindig," she said.

"I suppose it was a little too much . . ."

"Yes, it certainly *was* too much," said Madam Madsen in the same angry tone of voice.

It boiled up inside her more and more as she sat in the melancholy darkness in front of the pitiful, pale face on the pillows.

"No, I can see that," she repeated. "And he *deserved* it."

And she furiously told her everything: about Bai and about his maid at the inn and how long it had been going on . . .

"But Gusta didn't get off scot-free from it either . . ."

At first Katinka didn't understand a thing . . . she felt so heavy and listless.

Then she understood in a flash—and fixed her eyes on Madam Madsen's face for a moment.

"And you're killing yourself for a man like that," said Madam Madsen.

She was silent, waiting for Katinka to say something.

But Katinka lay there motionless. A few tears slid simply down her cheeks.

"Oh well," said Madam Madsen in a different voice, "probably no one else would have been much smarter."

Madam Madsen had gone.

"Marie," said Katinka, "draw the curtains so the light can come in."

Marie drew the curtains so the daylight fell across the bed.

"Why is the mistress crying?" she asked.

Katinka lay turned toward the light.

"Is it your lungs?" asked Marie.

"No, no," said Katinka. "I feel fine."

She kept on crying, soundlessly and happily.

Her weeping subsided and she lay there in the same position, exhausted, in indescribable peace.

Those were the last sunny days of autumn. In the bright mornings Katinka would lie indoors with the sun full on her bed. She made up so many happy dreams while her hands glided softly back and forth over the sun-warm blanket.

"The mistress looks so well," said Marie.

"Yes, I feel good too." She nodded without opening her eyes and lay still again, in the sunshine.

"Tomorrow I'll get up again," she said.

"Yes, the mistress can . . ."

Katinka turned toward the window. "It seems like summer," she said. "If I could go out tomorrow . . ."

She kept on talking about it—about whether she could go out. Down to the gazebo and the elder tree.

Did it still have leaves, the elder?—and the roses—and the cherry trees . . .

"Last year they were in bloom—a profusion of blossoms."

"The whole town got some for canning while the mistress was away," said Marie.

"The white blossoms . . ."

Katinka continued to talk about the garden. She kept saying, "Do you think he'll let me—that I'll be able to . . ."

"Maybe—if the sun is out."

The doctor did not come, and in the afternoon Marie had to go out to inquire.

It grew dark before Marie returned.

Katinka lay there without any light. She rang the little bell next to her bed.

"Hasn't she come back?" she asked.

"She had to walk the whole way," said Bai.

"How long it's taking," said Katinka. Fever flushed her cheeks.

She lay there, listening to every door that opened.

"The kitchen door just opened," she said.

"It was a man selling brooms," said Bai.

"She'll never come," said Katinka.

"You're going to make yourself sick again," said Bai.

She lay quietly, not ringing or speaking anymore. Then she heard Marie open the office door, and she lay with pounding heart under the blanket, without asking.

"What did he say?" asked Bai out there.

"Yes—for half an hour around noon," said Marie, "if the sun is out. Is the mistress asleep?"

"I think so."

Marie tiptoed in. Katinka lay quietly for a moment.

"Is that you?" she asked.

"Yes, the mistress can get up for a while and sit in the sunshine, he said, around noon."

Katinka did not answer at once. Then she took Marie's hand.

"Thank you," she said. "You're so kind, Marie."

"My mistress's hand is burning."

Katinka had a fever during the night; she lay with shining eyes and couldn't sleep. But she didn't wake Marie until morning.

Marie looked out the window in the parlor.

"It's going to be clear," she said. "Look at the weather."

"Look out the kitchen door," said Katinka from her bed. "There are always clouds there."

From the kitchen door it was clear too.

"I can do it myself, I can do it myself," said Katinka. She leaned against the walls in the hallway, over to the platform door.

"How warm it is," she said.

"Now come the stairs . . . so—I managed that . . ."

It was difficult walking on the gravel. She put her arm around Marie's shoulder. "My head feels so heavy," she said.

She stopped at every third step and looked out over the fields and off toward the woods. The sun seemed to have illuminated every single multicolored leaf.

Katinka wanted to go over to the platform gate. She paused for a moment, supporting herself.

"How beautiful it is," she said, "our little woods."

Katinka gazed far down the sunlit road. "Over there is the milestone," she said.

She turned her head and looked across the fields and the meadows and at the clear sky.

"Yes," she said, her voice quite soft, "it's so beautiful here."

Marie wiped her eyes whenever the mistress wasn't looking.

"But how the leaves are falling," said Katinka. She turned around and took a few steps on her own.

They went into the garden.

Katinka no longer spoke. They walked down the lawn to the gazebo.

"The elder," she simply said.

"I have to sit here," she said. Marie wrapped the blankets around her; huddled there, she gazed silently at the sunlit garden.

The leaves from the cherry trees lay yellow on the lawn; a couple of little roses were still in bloom.

Marie wanted to pick them.

"No," said Katinka, "that would be a shame—let them be."

She continued to sit there. Her lips moved, as if she were whispering.

"This is where Huus preferred to sit," said Marie. She was standing next to the bench.

Katinka gave a start. Then, smiling gently, she said: "Yes, he liked to sit here."

They walked on.

When they reached the gate, Katinka stood still for a moment. She looked back at the garden.

"I wonder who will walk there now?" she said.

She was so tired. She leaned heavily on Marie, and inside in the hallway she held on to the walls.

"Open the back door," she said, "so I can see the woods."

She went over and stood for a moment, leaning on the doorway and gazing out toward the woods and the road.

"Marie," she said, "I want to see the doves too . . ."

Katinka did not get up again. Her strength left her little by little.

Widow Abel brought her wine gelatin.

"To refresh your *tongue*," she said. She sat and looked at Katinka with tear-filled eyes.

"And you're lying here so *alone*," she said.

Mrs. Abel wanted to send over her Big Louise.

"She's like a *deaconess*," she said; her eldest, a deaconess . . .

Big Louise came in the morning and walked around on tiptoes, wearing a white apron. Katinka lay as if asleep. Big Louise set the breakfast table and brewed the coffee.

And the door to the bedroom was left ajar while they ate.

Bai was very grateful. The widow dried her eyes. "You have *friends* in misfortune," she said.

Mrs. Linde came in the afternoon and sat next to the bed knitting. She talked about new and old events in the entire region, and about herself and her Linde.

Old Linde came to get his wife at dusk, and the two old people sat by the bed for another hour in the twilight.

Agnes was the only thing on their minds.

"Linde can't live without Agnes," said Mrs. Linde. She herself shed tears in secret day and night.

"Yes, yes, my dear, she's the apple of my eye," said the old pastor.

"You'll see, she'll come back someday," said Katinka.

"As an old maid." Mrs. Linde's knitting needles clicked.

Mrs. Linde could not forget the part about "an old maid."

They sat and talked, and the old pastor had a black currant rum before he went home.

"It does a body good," he said, "and it doesn't go to your head."

The old folks shuffled home along the autumn-dark road.

Bai went out so regularly.

"A little *l'ombre* to cheer you up," said Kiær. "You need it, old friend."

"Yes, old Kiær." Bai put his hands over his eyes. "Sometime later in the week. Thanks a lot. Thanks for your friendship." He patted Kiær on the back, feeling moved. Bai was quite easily moved lately.

He went out and played *l'ombre* until late at night.

When he came home he woke up Katinka because he "couldn't go to bed without seeing how she was feeling."

"Fine, thank you," said Katinka. "Did you have fun?"

"As much as I could," said Bai, "with you lying here." He sat by the bed sighing for a while until he had made Katinka wide awake.

"Good night," he said then.

"Sleep well, Bai."

When Marie was out during the day, the doors stood open to the office. Katinka would lie there listening to the tap of the telegraph.

"How busy it is," she said. "How much it has to say."

"Bai," she called, "it's for here . . ."

Bai swore a high oath out in the office.

"Well—I'll be damned"—he appeared in the doorway—"it's for the Lindes."

"The Lindes?" Katinka sat up in bed. "It must be from Agnes."

Bai didn't reply, he was completely frantic; he ran around with the blue pencil and he had to find his jacket and he wrote the dispatch in his shirtsleeves, wrote it wrong, and tore it up.

"Bai," said Katinka, "Bai—is it Agnes?"

"I'll be damned."

Bai himself stormed off with the telegram, just as the afternoon train was about to arrive.

Bai had never seen such joy. The two old people laughed and cried.

"Oh God—can it be true—oh God—can it be true . . ."

"Yes—little mother—yes, yes . . ." The old pastor tried to be calm.

He shushed her and patted her on the head.

But then he folded his hands. "No," he said, "this is too much."

He wept too and dried his eyes with the velvet skullcap.

"Well, well," he said. "Praise be to God, I say; praise be to God . . ."

The old pastor wanted to take the news to Katinka himself, and he got out his coat and his hat and gloves and put them down again and took Bai's hands.

"Yes, the joy, Stationmaster," he said, "for us two old folks who sit here—to experience this . . . to experience this, Stationmaster."

"Hm—yes—everyone takes it in his own way . . ."

"Andersen had to learn to miss her, to really miss her," said the old pastor.

He puttered about and couldn't manage to leave.

The pastor's wife came in with strawberry liqueur before they got away.

The old pastor whistled "The Brave Soldier" as he walked along the road.

He sat inside next to Katinka's bed.

"Yes," he said, "God does lead the right people together."

A week later Agnes came home.

She stormed across the platform and through the office. In the office doorway she saw Katinka, who was lying on her pillow with her eyes closed. Agnes would not have recognized her.

Katinka opened her eyes and saw her.

"Yes," she said, "it's me."

Agnes went over and took Katinka's hands. She knelt down beside her bed.

"Lovely woman," said Agnes, fighting not to cry.

She came over every afternoon and sat with Katinka until evening.

They didn't talk much. Katinka dozed, and Agnes would let her sewing drop onto her lap and look at the pitiful face on the pillow. The feeble breathing whistled in Katinka's lungs.

Katinka moved and she would take up her sewing again and stick the needle in and out.

Katinka lay awake. She was so listless that she couldn't speak. The cough came and shook her; she sprang up in bed, as if she were going to be ripped apart.

Agnes held her up. Katinka was wet with cold sweat.

"Thank you," she said, "thank you."

She fell back again and lay still. From inside the bed curtains she saw Agnes's face, so round and strong, and her hands that moved so resolutely over her sewing.

"Agnes," she said, "won't you play a little?"

"You should sleep," said Agnes.

"Oh no, play a little."

Agnes got up and went out to the piano. Softly she played one melody after another.

Katinka lay still with her hands on the blanket.

"Agnes," she said, "sing it . . . won't you?"

It was the song about Sorrento. Agnes sang it in her dark alto voice:

> Where the tall and murky pine
> Lends its shadow to the peasant's vine,
> Where by the gulf the orange grove
> Smells so lovely in the evening mauve;
> Where by the strand the boat does rock,
> Where in the town the happy flock
> Dances while a song they raise,
> Singing loud the Madonna's praise.
> Never, never, shall I forget
> These hills and dales where once we met,
> These limpid moonlit nights,
> Napoli—your paradise.

She remained seated at the piano for a moment. Then she stood up and went into the bedroom.

"Thank you," said Katinka.

She lay in silence for a while.

"Yes," she said softly, "how beautiful life could be."

Agnes lay down on the bed. They lay there silently, both of them, in the darkness. Katinka's hand stroked Agnes's hair.

"Agnes," she said, "I don't want them—to read a sermon over me . . ."

"But Katinka . . ."

"Just a prayer," she said.

She was silent again. Agnes wept quietly. Katinka kept on curling little locks of her hair between her fingers.

"But there is," she said quite softly, and almost fearfully, and her hand fell away from Agnes's hair, "a hymn—that—that I would like to have sung . . . at my grave."

She was whispering almost inaudibly. Agnes lay with her head on the pillow.

"The wedding hymn," said Katinka very softly, like a child who didn't dare ask.

Sobs shook Agnes and she took Katinka's hands and kissed them as she wept.

"But Katinka—dear Katinka . . ."

Katinka took her head in her hands and leaned forward slightly.

"Now the two of you will be happy," she said.

She lay silent. Agnes continued to weep.

The next day Katinka was given the last rites by the old pastor. Bai was away in Randers.

Agnes was awakened in the night by a frightened maid with a candle: "There's a messenger, Miss—from the station . . . the mistress must come right away."

"A messenger?" Agnes was out of bed. "Who's here?" she asked.

She called down the hallway.

"Me," said Little Bentzen.

Agnes came out wrapped in several shawls.

"She's dying, Miss," said Little Bentzen. He stood there pale, his teeth chattering. Little Bentzen had never seen anyone die before.

"Did you send for the doctor?" asked Agnes. "The lantern, Ane."

"There was no one to go . . ."

Agnes lit the lantern and went across the courtyard. She pounded on the hired hands' door. It echoed off the barn.

"Lars, Lars . . ."

The horses began to stir in their stalls.

Lars appeared in the Dutch door, drunk with sleep, in the light of the lantern.

Agnes went back across the courtyard to the hall door. Little Bentzen had come out on the steps, afraid of standing in the dark.

"You're coming with me," said Agnes, walking by.

A couple of startled maids came out in the hall.

"Make some coffee," said Agnes. "Hurry up."

She went inside to get dressed. Little Bentzen was left alone in the hallway. The doors stood open throughout the house, creaking in the darkness. The maids were rustling around, half-dressed and heavy with sleep, each with a candle. They had forgotten a candlestick on the dining room table. The light flickered in the draft.

Out in the courtyard the boy came over with the stable lantern. He put it down on the cobblestones and went away— there was a circle of light around the lantern in the darkness.

The door to the stable was thrown open and they came out with the horses. Every sound was louder and more frightening in the night.

Agnes came out and passed Bentzen in the hallway.

"I'm going down there now," she said. "Is she having convulsions?"

"She was screaming," said Bentzen.

Agnes looked out into the courtyard. "Hurry up," she shouted. The boy ran across the courtyard with the lantern.

A couple of flickering candles were placed in the kitchen window so that their glow fell onto the horses and the wagon.

Old Mrs. Linde came into the dining room dressed in one

of the old pastor's bathrobes. "Stay in bed, Mother," said
Agnes.

"Oh, dear Lord. Oh, dear Lord," said old Mrs. Linde.
"So it came on suddenly... So it came on suddenly..." And
she began to walk around with a candle in her hand like the
others.

The boy threw open the gates—the noise made all of them
jump—and Lars appeared in the kitchen doorway and got a
bowl of coffee.

Little Bentzen came out and climbed onto the carriage
box. He saw Mrs. Linde's face—she was weeping and rocking
in the parlor in front of the flickering candle.

They rolled out of the gate, down the road, through the
darkness—at a trot so the willows of the hedgerow rushed
past them like dancing ghosts.

Lars gripped the reins hard.

"The beasts are skittish when you're driving toward
death," he said.

They did not speak again. The light from the carriage lanterns raced across the restless willows.

Bai was pacing back and forth in the front parlor, back and
forth along the wall.

"Is that you? Is that you?" he asked. "God, how she's
screaming."

Agnes opened the door to the office. She heard Katinka
gasping and the voice of the night nurse: "Now now, now
now..."

Marie came. "The doctor?" she asked.

"He's gone for him," said Agnes.

She went in. The nurse was holding Katinka's arms over
her head. Spasms tore through her body under the blankets.

"Hold here," said the nurse.

Agnes took her wrists and let them go again; she felt the cold sweat.

The dying woman struck out toward the bed curtains, her arms bent in convulsions.

"Hold on," said the nurse.

Agnes held her arms. "Her tongue, her tongue," she said. "Get a spoon, her tongue."

Katinka sank back—bluish-white foam crept out of her open lips through her clenched teeth.

Marie dropped the spoon and couldn't find it on the floor and rummaged around for another with the candle.

"Her head," said the nurse, "her head."

Marie held it, shaking all over. "Oh Jesus, oh, my sweet savior," she kept on saying. "Oh Jesus . . . oh . . . my sweet savior . . ."

Agnes pressed Katinka's arms down. "Her head back," said the nurse. She was almost lying down as she pressed the spoon between the dying woman's teeth.

Foam came out over the spoon. "Good," whispered the nurse, "good."

Katinka opened her eyes. Big and full of fear, they locked on Agnes.

Katinka kept staring at her with that same expression.

"Katinka . . ."

The dying woman moaned and sank back. The spoon fell out of her mouth.

"She'll have peace now," said the nurse.

Katinka's eyes fell shut. Agnes let go of her arms.

They sat down, each on one side of the bed, listening to her breathing, which came irregularly and quite faintly.

"She'll have peace now," said the nurse.

The dying woman dozed, moaning now and then.

The carriage arrived on the road outside. The door was opened and the doctor's voice was heard.

Agnes got up and shushed them.

"She's sleeping," she said.

The doctor went in and leaned over the bed. "Yes," he said, "it will be over soon."

"Is she suffering?" asked Agnes.

"We can't tell," said the doctor. "Now she's sleeping."

The doctor and Agnes sat down in the parlor. In the office they could hear Bai pacing up and down.

Agnes got up and went in.

"What does he say?" asked Bai. He continued to pace.

Agnes did not reply; she sat silently in her chair.

"I wouldn't have believed it," said Bai, "I wouldn't have believed it, Miss Agnes."

He wandered around, from the door to the window—and stopped again near Agnes's chair and said to himself: "I just wouldn't have believed it, Miss Agnes."

The doctor opened the door. "Come," he said.

The convulsions had started again. Bai was supposed to hold one of her arms.

But he let go of it again.

"I can't," he said and left with his face in his hands. They heard him sobbing in the office.

"Wipe her forehead," said the doctor.

Agnes wiped the sweat from her forehead.

"Thank you," said Katinka and opened her eyes. "Is that Agnes?"

"Yes, Katinka, it's Agnes."

"Thank you."

She dozed off again.

Toward morning she woke up. All of them were sitting by her bed.

Her eyes were glazed.

"Bai," she said.

"Yes."

"Ask her to play."

"Play," said the doctor.

Agnes went out. Tears ran down over the keys and her hands as she played without hearing her own notes.

Katinka lay quietly. Her breast rose and fell, whistling.

"Why isn't she playing?" she asked again.

"But she is playing, Tik . . ."

"She can't hear anymore."

The dying woman shook her head.

"I can't hear it," she said. "The hymn," she whispered, "the hymn."

She lay quietly again for a moment. The doctor sat taking her pulse and looking at her face.

Then she raised herself up and tore her hand away.

"Bai!" she screamed, "*Bai!*"

Agnes stood up and ran in. They were all standing around the bed. Bai knelt down and sobbed.

They all gave a start. It was the telegraph echoing through the rooms, announcing the train.

Katinka opened her eyes. "Look, look," she said, raising her head.

"Look at the sun," she said. "Look at the sun on the mountains."

She lifted her arms; they dropped again and slipped off the blanket.

The doctor quickly bent over the bed.

Agnes knelt at the foot with her head against the bed, next to Marie.

The only sound was a loud sobbing.

The doctor lifted the limp arms and folded the hands across the dead woman's breast.

"Hm, looks like you haven't slept much, Bentzen." Tight Pants jumped down from the train.

"How are things?"

"She's dead," said Little Bentzen; he spoke as if he were freezing.

"What?—The devil . . ."

Tight Pants stood there for a moment, looking at the little station building: everything was the same as usual.

Then he turned around and quietly climbed onto the step.

The train was hidden by the winter mists over the fields.

Chapter Seven

I t was the first day of winter. Clear sky and a thin layer of snow on the lightly frozen earth.

Outside the church the men had begun to assemble, solemn, with tall silk hats of various vintages. They whispered in small groups, and one by one they went over and peered down into the empty grave close to the wall.

Inside the church four or five silent women were up by the casket, quietly arranging the wreaths. The parish clerk and Little Jensen were placing the hymnals on the chairs.

They were finished. "And number 753 in the hymnal at the graveside," said Little Jensen.

Little Jensen was a kind of undertaker when the "occasion" demanded it. She had immediately taken over the body, both at home and in the church. The "Instityoot" had had "fall vacation" ever since the death.

Miss Jensen looked around the church and went up toward the casket with the parish clerk. The garlands were hanging in uniform loops above the chancel, and the black mourning crêpe had been draped like two sausages over the altar candlesticks.

"Lovely casket for this time of year," said the parish clerk.

They stood and looked at the wreaths.

"They make beautiful wreaths at the miller's," said Little Jensen.

"You can certainly tell the difference," said the parish clerk, shrugging his shoulders and looking at the wreath from the Abels.

"Yes," said Miss Jensen, "they don't take any *interest*."

Miss Jensen moved away a little and assessed the casket.

"Yes," she said, "I'm glad we took the oak."

"It is, if I may say so, also better for the body," said the parish clerk.

The bells began to ring, and Miss Jensen went out to the cemetery. She greeted the parents of her pupils and took a head count.

Bai came in through the gate with two gentlemen wearing footwarmers; all the hats were lifted. Little Jensen shook hands in the entryway.

When everyone was seated, the Abel family arrived. The widow was in the lead; it looked as if she had been in a rush. The two chicks wore veils of mourning like two widows.

Big Louise placed an ivy cross on the casket.

Agnes was sitting next to the old pastor. She didn't hear the song and did not open her hymnal. She just sat and stared with moist eyes at the lovely woman's casket.

The song died out. The old pastor stood up and walked forward.

When Bai saw him standing there with folded hands in front of the casket, he burst into tears and sobbed.

The old pastor waited quietly, with his eyes on the casket. His voice was muted when he spoke. The winter sun fell in through the chancel windows onto the casket and flowers.

The old pastor spoke about the quite people of the land.

"Quiet she was—quiet in her life; quietly she wanted to be brought to her final rest. The Lord God, who knows His own, gave her a life of happiness with a good husband; He gave her a death in peace by His Holy Spirit. May He receive her soul, He who alone knows the hearts and reins; may He grant His solace, the only Consoler—to those who now grieve."

"Amen."

Old Linde was silent. It was completely still.

The pallbearers stepped forward with the parish clerk and Little Jensen, who pulled the wreaths from the casket.

And all of them, standing up at their places, gazed after the casket which was carried out with the song:

> It is so lovely to walk together
> For two who gladly their life would share.
> Then they with joy are doubly blessed
> And halve the sorrow, so hard to bear.
> > Yes, it is joyous
> > To walk together
> > When the plumage
> > Is truly love.

Agnes continued to gaze after the casket. The doors were thrown wide open to the bright day.

> Is truly love . . .

They had reached the grave. The pallbearers had to walk over the rough ground with the casket; the grave digger dropped the rope and it fell into the grave.

Everyone stood there waiting for them to get hold of the rope end and throw the rope around the casket.

Bai was holding on to a shrub as if he were going to break it. The rope tightened as the casket was pushed out and sank.

Agnes had closed her eyes.

> It is so sad to have to part
> For those who gladly their life would share,
> But God be praised: in our Lord's abode
> Forever gather the lovers fair.
> > Yes, it is joyous
> > To live together
> > Where hearth and home
> > Are truly love.

"Now, now, brother-in-law." The two men in footwarmers supported Bai, who was sobbing.

The song died away. It was silent, not a sound; not a breeze over the bare heads.

The sand fell heavily from old Linde's shaking hands.

Our Father, who art in heaven . . .

It was over. The two men in the footwarmers shook hands and thanked everyone for "their great sympathy."

Mrs. Abel stopped them at the gate. She had her little table laid for Bai and his brothers-in-law.

"In all modesty—so you won't be alone . . ."

Mrs. Abel wiped her eyes.

"A woman knows what it is to lose someone," she said.

The crowd was gone.

Agnes stood alone at the grave. She gazed down at the casket with its wreaths, spotted with sand.

And she stared out over the roads, where all the people were walking home to life again.

There was Bai between the two women dressed in mourning—the long veils—and the two men in the footwarmers. They were Katinka's brothers, who had thanked everyone on the family's behalf.

Little Jensen was going to have dinner at the miller's after her exertions. Miss Helene was suffering in boots that were too small.

There they went, all of them . . .

And they were hurrying.

Agnes bowed her head. She felt an angry dislike for this petty life that was rushing on home down all the roads.

Someone came up behind her. It was Little Bentzen with a large box.

"It's a wreath, Miss," he said. "I wanted to bring it myself. It came on the noon train."

Little Bentzen took the wreath out of the box.

"It's from Huus," he said.

"From Huus," said Agnes. She took the wreath and looked at the half-withered roses. "How beautiful it was."

"Yes," said Bentzen. "It was pretty once."

They stood there for a moment. Agnes knelt halfway down and let the wreath slide gently down onto the casket. The rose petals were scattered in the fall.

When Agnes turned around, Little Bentzen was standing there crying.

A man came over to them.

"If the Miss—we're going to close . . ."

"Yes, we're coming. The parish clerk would probably give me permission to be here," said Agnes.

Agnes and Bentzen walked silently along the path. The hired hand was already waiting to close the gate.

With her hands in her coat pockets, Agnes stood and watched the man close the gate and padlock it.

Little Bentzen was still sniffling as he left with a goodbye.

Agnes remained standing in front of the locked gate.

Bai was frequently over at the Abels'.

Mrs. Abel couldn't stand the thought of him sitting down there, alone, in the desolate house . . . "When we're sitting by a cozy lamp," said Mrs. Abel.

She and her Big Louise came to get him after the 8 o'clock train.

"Let's just go home to the lamp," said Mrs. Abel.

Big Louise was quite at home at the station. She had to water the flowers in a hurry before they left.

Mrs. Abel stood nearby.

"They were her favorites, the dear," she said mildly.

"The dear" was Katinka.

"But the hanging flowerpot," said Big Louise. "It's thirsty too." She nodded toward the hanging plant.

Bai had to hold the chair whenever Big Louise watered the hanging plant. She stood on her toes with the watering can and displayed her beauty.

"She doesn't forget a thing," said Mrs. Abel. The hanging flowerpot was watered so that it splashed onto the floor.

"Marie will wipe it up," said Big Louise sharply out in the kitchen. She always stood for a moment in the pantry doorway and "supervised." Big Louise had such nimble fingers whenever something sweet had been left on a saucer.

They went home to the lamp.

Big Louise poured the tea wearing a white apron.

They had to call and call for Little Ida.

"She's *writing*," said the widow from her corner.

Little Ida was always writing in an odd, half-clothed state.

"Bosse-Sa has forgotten her cuffs," said the widow.

"Oh," said Bosse-Sa. Bosse-Sa was generally in disarray.

"*He's* not here, you know," said the widow.

After tea Bai would have his toddy with *The Daily Telegraph*. Big Louise embroidered. The widow sat and looked "tender."

"You must make yourself at home. That's all we want."

When Bai was done with the paper, Big Louise would play. She finished with one of Katinka's little melodies.

"She played that one, the dear," said the widow and looked at her portrait. Katinka hung with a wreath of *immortelle* beneath the mirror above the sofa.

"Yes," said Bai. He was sitting with his hands folded. By the lamp, after his toddy, Bai always felt a mild emotion about his "loss."

The widow *understood* him.

"But one has the transfigured memory," she said. "And the reunion."

"Yes."

Bai wiped his two fingers across his eyes.

They spoke of the "dear departed" while Bai had his second glass.

Little Jensen sat in the dark at her window in order to hear when he left.

Little Jensen was mostly at the parsonage lately.

"At the Abels' they aren't too fond of being disturbed," said Little Jensen.

Miss Jensen had been at the station often during the first weeks after the death.

"A woman helps out where she can," she told the millers.

"That's right," said the miller's wife.

Miss Helene stretched out her legs and looked at her felt slippers.

"And that dear Katinka"—Miss Jensen called her Katinka after her death—"has *spoiled* him."

Little Jensen assumed a kind of supervisory role at the station.

"What good is it to have a maid?" she said.

She came after school hours with a basket and Bel-Ami. Bel-Ami had his own basket next to the stove.

She went about in silence and made his favorite dishes.

When the table was set, she had her coat on. Bai begged her to stay and have a bite of food with him.

"All right, if you'd rather that I stayed," said Little Jensen. "I'm a living creature, at least," she said modestly.

Bel-Ami was put back in his place, and they ate.

Little Jensen did not intrude with conversation. She sat there like a silent participant while Bai helped himself to his favorite dishes. He had begun to get his appetite back.

After dinner they would play a taciturn game of *piquet*.

At ten o'clock Miss Jensen would leave.

"I was over at the grave," she said, "with a flower."

Miss Jensen tended the grave.

She listened to Bel-Ami howl as she walked along the road toward home. She didn't pick him up.

Miss Jensen walked deep in thought. She was thinking of selling her school.

She had always been better suited to a position where a woman with education was like the mistress of the house.

But in the last two or three months Miss Jensen had not been to the station very often.

She didn't like being considered one of the pushy ones.

She didn't *understand* Mrs. Abel at all.

In the evening she would sit by the window to hear whether he even managed to escape back home.

"I tend the *grave*," she said at the miller's.

"Damn these women the way they bustle about." In the office Kiær swatted the air with his hat as if trying to keep the flies away. Big Louise had slipped past him in the doorway.

"Damn all this bustling about," said Kiær.

Kiær was going to Copenhagen and wanted to take Bai along.

"You need to get out, old boy, you really need it . . . Get some fresh air in your lungs. You old bachelor . . . Out on the *bowling* green," he said.

Bai couldn't make up his mind. "You know—so soon after." But get some fresh air in his lungs—that he could do.

A week later they left. Mrs. Abel and Big Louise packed his suitcase.

Bai stretched himself on the seat and flexed his arm muscles as they rolled off.

"Taking a trip?" said Tight Pants. They ran into him at a station.

"A bachelor's junket . . . Two happy young roosters . . ." Tight Pants laughed and snapped his tongue with a pop.

Bai said, "Yes, we're going in to see how it wiggles."

He slapped Kiær on both knees and repeated: "Wiggles, old man . . ."

They rolled off and waved to Tight Pants, who shouted after them.

Suddenly they grew quite lively, using vulgar words and slapping their legs.

"So we're off again, one more time," said Bai.

"What are we here for, us human beings?" said Kiær.

"*Adam*, old man," said Bai.

They laughed and talked. Kiær was happy.

"Now you're your old self again," he said. "You old lamp polisher . . . Now you're yourself again."

Bai grew suddenly serious. "Yes, old friend," he said, "these have been sad times."

He sighed twice and leaned back a little against the seat.

Then he said in a happy voice again: "Hey—let's take Nielsen along."

"What Nielsen?" asked Kiær.

"A little lieutenant, a connoisseur . . . We don't know the new places, after all, old man. Met him at the parsonage . . . lively fellow . . . a connoisseur . . ."

"If there's going to be a party . . ."

They started yawning and quieted down; they fell asleep in their seats and slept until Fredericia.

There they drank some quick cognacs against the "night chill."

Bai went out on the platform. The cars were being shunted and there were bells ringing and whistles blowing so you couldn't hear a thing.

Bai stood under a lantern in the midst of the throng and let himself be shoved about.

"Old man," he said to Kiær, rubbing his hands as he looked down the platform and the track, "what do you think?"

"It's life, all right," said Kiær.

The ladies were nipping up and down the stairs, flushed with sleep under their traveling bonnets.

"And these *women*," said Bai.

There was yelling and shoving.

"Passengers for Strib—passengers for the ferry . . ."

Bai arrived in Copenhagen with the 10:30 train.

They found Lieutenant Nielsen on the fifth floor on Dannebrogsgade. His furniture consisted of a wardrobe with a broken door, which revealed a single uniform vest, and a cane-backed chair with a wash basin.

The lieutenant was lying in bed on a straw mattress.

"Field quarters," he said. "A man has his stateroom *else-where*, Stationmaster."

Bai told him that they wanted to "see" the town.

"Those kinds of places," he said, "you know..."

Lieutenant Nielsen *understood*.

"You have to see the market," he said. "Trust me: we have to see the market."

He got into his trousers and started yelling for a Madam Madsen. Madam Madsen stuck a piece of soap in through the doorway with a bare arm.

"It's just like a family," said the lieutenant. He soaped up his arms with Madam Madsen's soap.

They agreed on a place where they would meet to have a look at the casino's dancing legs. "And then we'll see the market," said Bai.

The lieutenant hit Madam Madsen up for 10 øre and then drove straight out to "the Pub."

The Pub was a nice little beer garden on Pileallé where "the group" gathered for ninepins and cards.

The group consisted of three second lieutenants and two towheaded men from the agricultural school.

When Nielsen arrived, the men were already playing *l'ombre* in their shirtsleeves with their hats pushed back.

"So—the twins," said Nielsen.

"How's it going?"

"We're watered down," said one of the towheads with a shrug.

"*Buoyantly,*" said one of the lieutenants.

"Quite *buoyantly*," said the other.

The group thrived on the word "buoyantly." They repeated it all around every quarter of an hour in an odd tone of voice with little waves of their hands.

"Buoyantly."

"You *have* to get watered down," said Nielsen.

The group got "watered down" with beer and "females."

"I've nabbed a couple of big spenders," said Nielsen.

"Big spenders—what the devil, Nielsen?" The towheaded men shoved their hats back.

"A couple of older big spenders, twins . . ."

The twins pounded the table with their beer bottles in honor of the discoverer.

They showed up in the evening at "the Coffin" after Nielsen had looked at "dancing legs" with Kiær and Bai.

Nielsen found a couple of ruddy-cheeked girls who drank Swedish punch with them and slapped "the two elderly gentlemen from the provinces" coquettishly on the fingers.

Bai said "premier" and other old-fashioned words from his lieutenant days.

The two towheaded men could never hold much. They sat there lolling and said: "You old pigs' bristles," lurching against Bai and Kiær.

They all kept on drinking.

"Oh, you old boot."

"Get your hands off me." Bai was getting sensitive from all the drinking.

Bai didn't know how it happened. The lieutenants had suddenly disappeared with the ruddy-cheeked women.

"They've flown the coop," said Kiær.

"The two gentlemen are sitting here all alone . . ."

It was an older little woman who was poking her nose over at their table.

A week had passed.

Kiær had business in the mornings. Bai slept most of the time.

Kiær came home, into the room.

"What, are you sleeping?" he said.

"Yes, I just don't feel good," said Bai on the sofa, rubbing his eyes. "What time is it?"

"Two."

"Then we have to get going." Bai got up from the sofa. "It's a damned ironing board," he said. All his limbs were sore. He managed to get dressed.

They were going to look for a gravestone. Bai wanted to buy Katinka's gravestone in Copenhagen.

He had gone to three or four stonecutters and hadn't been able to make up his mind.

Kiær was a little impatient about being dragged around among all those stones.

"It's nice of you, old friend—it's very nice of you . . . But it really makes no difference to her."

Bai was almost moved as he walked around among all those crosses and pillars with the marble doves and the angel heads.

Today he would have to decide, the last day.

He bought a large gray cross with a pair of marble hands that were clasped in a handshake beneath the butterfly of life.

Bai stood for a long time in front of the cross with the two hands and the butterfly.

"A beautiful thought," he said and rubbed his fingers over his eyes. "Faith, Hope, and Charity."

Kiær didn't always understand what Bai meant when he was grieving. "Yes, nice thought," he said.

They went to the Royal Theater in the evening. After the performance they were going out drinking.

"I say 'no thanks,' " said Kiær, "to warming a bench and waiting for that crowd." Kiær went home.

Bai took off alone. They wouldn't be able to say that *he* didn't keep at it till the very end.

He went into a tavern. None of the group had arrived, and he sat upstairs in the gallery and waited.

"No, thanks." He didn't want anything . . . "A seltzer."

He sat there looking down at the room through the tobacco smoke at the eight girls who were sitting on the stage in a semicircle, and at the spectators.

"Nothing but boys . . ."

Embezzlers, thought Bai. He sat there watching with his head leaning on his hand. "Boys," he repeated.

There were shouts and walking-sticks pounding down below: it was an English dancer who was energetically throwing her skirts up over her head. Bai had seen those skirts fly every evening.

And almost with ill-temper he looked down at the walking-stick enthusiasm.

"Is that anything to stomp for?" he said.

He gulped down the seltzer and continued to watch the room: the eight girls sitting in a row like sleepy hens on a perch and the boys cheering to make themselves believe that it was *fun*.

He had waited almost forty-five minutes, and the group hadn't arrived.

In fact, he didn't mind if they didn't show up—with their ruddy-cheeked girls.

He could probably find some old "virgin" himself . . .

Those two hicks with their "old pigs' bristles."

Bai looked over toward the other side: a couple of young men were flirting with two girls. One of them was young and fresh, with two little dimples . . . The young man leaned over and stole a kiss from under her veil.

The group still didn't show up. And Bai felt almost a kind of bitterness, *indignation,* as he kept watching those two doves billing and cooing.

No one came.

So—after they've fleeced you . . .

And the pub began to empty out. It was thinning out on the floor, couple after couple disappearing down the stairs from the gallery.

The smoke and the smell of beer lay thick and heavy over the tables full of abandoned glasses.

Up in the gallery only an older woman minced back and forth, nodding seductively at Bai.

They had already turned down the gaslight halfway, and Bai was still sitting with his head in his hands and staring at the desolate, filthy room.

He gave a curse when he stood up.

The older woman was bustling about at the gate.

"The gentleman is still here," she said.

"Never! To hell with you."

Bai poured all of his bitterness into the shove that he gave the older woman.

"What," whined the woman, "is that the way you treat a lady? . . . a homeowner? . . ."

Kiær was in bed.

"Well," he said, "did you have fun?"

Bai took off his boots.

"They never showed up," he said in a low voice.

"Riffraff," said Kiær.

Bai got undressed without speaking.

He lay there for a while next to the lit candle. Then he put it out.

"Are you angry, old man?" asked Kiær.

"No . . ."

"Well . . . good night."

"But a man's starting to get old," said Bai. "Yes," he said slowly, "that's the thing of it."

Kiær turned over in bed. "Rubbish," he said. "But you're taking it too hard, old man . . . You need some practice, you young rooster—and take it easy . . .

"Then you can cultivate it," he said. "Comfortably."

Kiær fell silent. A little later he was snoring. But Bai

couldn't fall asleep. He thought he could smell the stench of beer half the night, and he lay there tossing and turning.

Next morning, when he was packing his suitcase, the photograph of Katinka fell out from between two handkerchiefs.

It was Mrs. Abel who had given it to him to take along.

She had looked at it tenderly and wrapped it in tissue paper.

"The dear," she had said.

Big Louise, "my last one," had been cross: "Phooey—don't you think he should take a music box along . . . to play the 'dear melodies' . . ."

Louise, her last one, had a bad habit of sneering at her mother whenever something didn't go her way.

The widow had quietly placed the portrait in between two handkerchiefs.

"He should have this piece of home to take along . . ."

Bai picked up the portrait from the floor and sat down and looked at it with swimming eyes.

The Abel family was at the station to meet Bai. The rooms were Easter-clean and shining. With white curtains and the smell of cleaning.

Bai sat on the sofa for dinner.

"A man comes home to his domesticity. Home to the nest."

He ate and drank as if he hadn't had food on the whole trip.

Widow Abel had moist eyes from sitting and looking so lovingly at "our returnee."

He told them about the trip.

"The theaters," said the widow.

The season.

The gravestone he had bought . . . the devil of a price . . .

"You don't think about that," said the widow, "the last act of love."

"Yes, that was it"—he had said it to Kiær—"the last act of love," said Bai.

There was no end to Big Louise's little surprises. "Don't look," she said, putting her hands over his eyes while the widow took the lid off the last ragout dish.

"Yes, see what she's made," said the widow, smiling. "My eldest."

"Everyone is a homebody," said Bai. He put both hands on the table and looked happily around him as he relaxed.

It was October.

The platform was quite full for the afternoon train. Little Jensen and all of the Lindes and the folks from the mill.

The widow was leaving in order to set up house for Ida, her youngest.

"Louise will come later," she said and took her eldest's head in her hands. "She's a homebody."

"She won't come until the wedding," she said.

The wedding was going to be at the home of "my sister, the Councilor's wife."

"That's where they found each other," said the widow.

The train was announced; Bai came with a baggage claim check and a ticket.

"He's been my *salvation*," said the widow, nodding to him.

The train came down across the meadow.

"Say hello to Ida," said the old pastor. "We'll be thinking about her on that day."

"We know you will," said the widow. "We know where the kind thoughts are." She was moved and gave everyone a kiss.

"Yes," she said, "this is a journey to lose someone . . ."

The train arrived. "Well, dear Mrs. Abel," said Bai. "It's time."

"And—my Louise . . ."

"They'll take care of her." Bai had already put her into the compartment.

"Goodbye, Mrs. Linde . . . goodbye . . ."

Louise jumped up onto the train step and kissed her.

"My last," she said. "Louise!" cried the widow. The train had begun to move.

Bai caught Louise, her last one . . .

Everyone waved and waved, until they couldn't see the train anymore.

The Lindes walked home along the road with the people from the mill.

Big Louise wanted to put something in the mail bag and ran into the office ahead of Bai. They were laughing in there so you could hear it out on the platform.

Little Jensen was daydreaming, leaning against a post. The station hand had taken away the milk cans from the platform and switched the track. And Miss Jensen was still standing there, alone, leaning against the post.

The Lindes were home.

The old pastor was sitting with Agnes in the parlor while "Mother" looked after the tea.

It was twilight. The old pastor could barely see Agnes as she sat at the piano.

"Would you sing something?" he asked.

For a moment Agnes let her hands slide slowly up and down the keyboard. Then she sang in a low voice, in her dark alto, the song about Marianna:

> Beneath the turf of the grave sleeps
>   Poor Marianna—
> The girls come and they weep
>   for poor Marianna.

It was silent in the dark room.

The old pastor dozed a little over his folded hands.